"Staging some kind of Valentine vendetta! Which I presume is what you want me to do?"

"Maybe."

Fran stared down at the silver gleam of the high-tech table, and thought of rich Sam Lockhart luring decent, hardworking girls like Rosie to his bed. When she eventually lifted her golden-brown head to meet her friend's eyes, her own were deadly serious.

"What do you want me to do?" she asked at last.

Rosie didn't even have to think about it. "Nothing too major." She shrugged. "I'm not asking you to break any laws for me, Fran."

"What, then?"

"Just pay him back."

SHARON KENDRICK was born in west London, England, and has had heaps of jobs, which include photography, nursing, driving an ambulance across the Australian desert and cooking her way around Europe in a converted double-decker bus! Without a doubt, writing is the best job she's ever had, and when she's not dreaming up new heroes (some of which are based on her doctor husband) she likes cooking, reading, theater, listening to American West Coast music and talking to her two children, Celia and Patrick.

SHARON KENDRICK

Valentine Vendetta

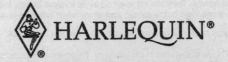

TORONTO • NEW YORK • LONDON
AMSTERDAM • PARIS • SYDNEY • HAMBURG
STOCKHOLM • ATHENS • TOKYO • MILAN • MADRID
PRAGUE • WARSAW • BUDAPEST • AUCKLAND

To the only other literary agent as
gorgeous as Sam Lockhart,
the inestimable and inspirational
Giles Gordon

ISBN 0-373-12084-2

VALENTINE VENDETTA

First North American Publication 2000.

Copyright © 1999 by Sharon Kendrick.

This edition published by arrangement with Harlequin Books S.A.

® and TM are trademarks of the publisher. Trademarks indicated with
® are registered in the United States Patent and Trademark Office, the
Canadian Trade Marks Office and in other countries.

Visit us at www.romance.net

Printed in U.S.A.

CHAPTER ONE

'FRAN—I'm at my wit's end! She seems to be having some kind of mid-life crisis!'

'But she's only twenty-six,' said Fran.

'*Exactly!*'

The memory of that phone call still burned in Fran's ears. A dramatic phone call, from a woman not given to dramatization.

'Just go and see her, would you, Fran?' Rosie's mother had pleaded. 'Something has happened to upset her and I can't get any sense out of her. But I suppose you girls don't tell your mothers anything.'

'So you've no idea what's wrong?' Fran had probed, thinking that it was rather flattering to be called a girl at the ripe old age of twenty-six!

'I think it has to do with some man—'

'Oh,' said Fran drily. 'The usual story.'

'And that life isn't worth living any more.'

'She said *what*?' That had been the statement which had brought Fran up short and had her booking the next London-bound flight out of Dublin. Not that she believed for a minute that Rosie would do anything *stupid*—but she was normally such a happy-go-lucky person. For her mother to be this worried, things must be bad.

Now she could see for herself that they were worse than bad.

She had found Rosie curled up like a baby on the sofa of one very cold flat. And the conversation had gone round and round in a loop, consisting of Rosie saying,

'Oh, Fran. Fran! *Fran!*' Followed by a renewed bout of shuddering tears.

'Sssh, now. It's all right.' Fran squeezed her friend's shoulder tightly as the tears came thick and fast. 'Why don't you take a deep breath, calm down and tell me what's wrong.'

Rosie made a sound like a cat who was trying to swallow a mouse in one. 'C-c-can't!' she shuddered.

'Off the top of my head, I'd say it's a man?' said Fran, thinking that it might be wise not to mention the worried phone call. Not just yet.

Rosie nodded.

'So tell me about him.'

'He's….he's…*oh!*'

'He's what?' prompted Fran softly.

'He's a bastard—and I still love him!'

Fran nodded. So. As she had thought. The usual story. She'd heard women pour the same sorry tale out countless times before and the more cruel the man, the more they seemed to love him. She wondered if some women were so lacking in self-esteem that they chose someone who would walk all over them. But she wouldn't have put *Rosie* in that category. 'Oh, I see.'

'No, you don't, Fran!' Rosie shook her head in frustration. 'You say you do but you don't! How could anyone see? You just sit there with that seen-it-all-before look on your face—'

'I've never seen *you* like this before,' Fran disagreed immediately. 'And I've known you most of your life! And before you insult me much more, Rosie Nichols— I might just remind you that I've flown over at top speed from Dublin, in answer to an urgent request from your mother that I find out exactly what's wrong with you.'

'My mother asked you to come?'

'She wasn't interfering, if that's what you're thinking. She was just worried, and wanted me to see how you were.'

Rosie looked at her defiantly. 'So now you know.'

Fran shook her head. 'Oh, no,' she corrected grimly. 'I haven't even started yet! All I know is that I walk into your flat which looks as though a major war has broken out—to find you sitting in a pathetic heap looking gaunt and tear-stained—sobbing bitterly about some mystery man whose name you can't bring yourself to utter—'

'Sam,' sniffed Rosie. 'His name is Sam.'

'Sam!' echoed Fran with a ghost of a smile. 'That's Sam whose paternity you questioned just a minute ago, is it? And does this Sam have a surname?'

'It's Lockhart.' Rosie looked at her expectantly. 'Sam Lockhart.'

'Sam Lockhart.' Fran considered this. 'Cute name. Catchy.'

'You haven't heard of him?'

'No. Should I have done?'

'Maybe not. But he's rich and gorgeous and those kind of attributes tend to get you known—especially among women.'

'Tell me more.'

Rosie shrugged her shoulders morosely. 'He's a literary agent. The best. They say if Sam takes you on, you're almost certain to end up living in tax-exile! He's got an instinctive nose for a best seller!'

Fran tried not to look too disapproving. 'And I suppose he's married?'

'*Married?* You're kidding!' Rosie shook her head so that wild curls spilled untidily around her face. 'What do you take me for?'

Fran breathed a sigh of relief. 'Well, he's not *completely* bad, then,' she said. 'Married men who play away from home are the worst. And *I* should know!' She flicked Rosie another look. 'Has he ever been married?'

Rosie shook her head. 'No, he's single. Still single,' she added, and stared down at her chewed fingernails as tears began to splash uninhibitedly onto her hands.

Fran gave Rosie's shoulder another squeeze. 'Want to tell me all about it?'

'I guess,' said Rosie listlessly.

'How long since you've eaten?'

Rosie shrugged. 'I had coffee for breakfast—but there's nothing much in the flat.'

Resisting the urge to remark that judging by the general air of neglect any food would probably carry a health warning, Fran shook her head. 'Don't be silly,' she said gently. 'I'm taking you out for dinner.'

Rosie momentarily brightened until she caught sight of herself in the mirror. 'But I can't go out looking like this!'

'Too right—you can't,' agreed Fran calmly. 'So go and do something to your hair, slap on some warpaint and for goodness sake, *lose* those hideous baggy trousers!'

An hour later, they were installed in a booth at 'Jacko's!'—a restaurant/bar which had just opened up on the water's edge at one of London's less fashionable riverside locations. It had the indefinable buzz of success about it. Fran smiled up at the waitress whose skirt barely covered her underwear and ordered two alien-sounding cocktails from the menu.

She stared across the table at Rosie whom she had known since they were both fat-faced three-year-olds toddling into school on their first day at Nursery, where Rosie had demonstrated her ability for attracting trouble by losing her teddy bear down the side of a bookcase. And Fran had slipped her small hand in and retrieved it.

It had set a pattern for their school years. Rosie got herself into a scrape and Fran got her out of it! Since Fran had moved to Dublin five years ago, their paths rarely crossed, but after a few minutes back in her old friend's company, Fran felt as if they'd never been apart.

Well, maybe not quite.

Rosie seemed terribly distracted, jumpy even—but maybe in the circumstances that was understandable. Her face looked harder, too. But Fran told herself that people changed—she had changed herself. She had had to. That was all part of life's rich tapestry. Or so they said....

'Now tell me,' she said firmly. 'Just who Sam Lockhart *is*—and why you've fallen in love with him.'

'Oh, everyone falls in love with him!' Rosie gave a gloomy shrug. 'You can't help yourself.'

'Then it's a pity *I* can't meet him,' observed Fran. 'Since that sounds like the sort of challenge it would give me great pleasure to resist!'

'I'd like to see you try!'

Fran liberated a smooth strand of hair which had somehow become all twisted up in the string of pearls she wore and fixed her friend with a stern expression. 'In my earlier life as an agony aunt on a well-known Dublin radio station,' she said, 'I soon learnt that the easiest way to forget a man is to start thinking of him as a mere mortal and not as a god. Debunk the myth, that's what I say!'

Rosie screwed her nose up. 'Come again?'

'Stop making everything about him seem so wonderful and extraordinary—'

'But it is!'

Fran shook her head. 'That's the wrong way to look at it. Try concentrating on all the *bad* things about him instead!'

'Like what?'

'Well, I don't know the man, so I can't really help you with that. But instead of describing him as, say, utterly unobtainable, tell yourself that he's arrogant and distant and nobody in their right mind would want to live with him! Right?'

'Er, right,' said Rosie doubtfully.

Fran winced as a silver beaker of what looked and smelt like cough medicine was placed in front of her. She took a tentative sip through the straw and nearly shot off the edge of her seat before a dreamy kind of lethargy began to melt her bones. Still, some light anaesthetic might be just what Rosie needed.

'Drink up,' she instructed and leaned forward eagerly as she began to slide the drink across the table towards Rosie. 'And tell me what happened. Like—where did you meet him?'

Rosie took a quick slug of the cocktail. 'Remember when I did that stint as a secretary for Gordon-Browne—that big firm of literary agents? Well, Sam was their star player and we got kind of, you know…involved.'

Fran nodded, thinking how unusually coy Rosie sounded. 'So how long did it last?'

'Er, not as long as I would have liked.'

'And when did it end?'

'Oh, ages ago now,' gulped Rosie vaguely. 'Months and months. Longer, even. Over two years,' she admitted at last.

'Two *years*?' Fran blinked. 'But surely you should be getting over it by now?'

'Why?' Rosie sniffed. 'How long did it take you to get over the breakup of your marriage to Sholto?'

'Oh, no.' Fran shook her head. 'We're here to talk about you, not me. Surely you haven't been like this since it ended?'

Rosie shook her head. 'No, of course I haven't—but my life has never been the same since Sam. He brought me bad luck. I haven't been able to settle into another job *or* another relationship. And now I've heard....' Her voice tailed off into silence.

Fran hoped to high heaven that this man Sam hadn't done something like announcing his engagement to someone else. That would be hard. Though maybe a brutal demonstration of his love for someone else might be just the cure that Rosie actually needed. 'Heard what?' she asked.

'He's planning to throw a ball. Which is *totally* out of character!'

Which immediately told Fran that he must be rich. And well connected. 'And?'

'It's a Valentine's Day Ball. And I want to be invited,' said Rosie fiercely.

'Well, you might be. Don't you think?'

'No, I don't. But I would, wouldn't I—if *you* were organizing it! You'd make sure of that!' Rosie's eyes took on a hopeful gleam.

Fran shook her head as she saw which way the conversation was heading. 'Oh, no!'

'Fran, it's your job! That's what you do for a living, you plan people's parties for them.'

'Yes, you're right, I do. But it's also my livelihood, Rosie, and I have my reputation to think of. Huge, high-profile society balls aren't really my thing. And I don't just go around using these events to settle grudges for friends—however much I love them. Staging some kind of Valentine vendetta! Which I presume is what you want me to do. Or is it just an invitation you're after? You want to dress to kill and then knock his socks off, is that it?'

'Maybe.'

Fran gave a wistful smile. 'It won't work, you know. It never does. If this man Sam has fallen out of love with you—then nothing you can say or do will bring him back. Nothing,' she emphasised flatly. 'That's life, I'm afraid.'

Rosie bit down on her lip. 'But he never *was* in love with me.'

'Oh. Oh, I see.' Fran's eyes softened. 'Well, in that case I'm very sorry, hon,' she said gently. 'What can I say?'

Rosie took a mouthful of Fran's discarded cocktail, then looked up, her eyes two fierce burning stars in her face. 'I was just another virgin for Sam to seduce,' she said dully. 'To pick up and discard once he'd had what he wanted!'

Something primitive cracked like an old bone inside Fran's head. She remembered their schoolgirl dreams about men and rice and white dresses and knew she should not be shocked at what Rosie had just told her—certainly not in this day and age, and yet she *was* shocked. Deeply. 'He took your virginity?' she said slowly. 'Did he *know*?'

'Yes, of course he knew.' Rosie gave a cynical laugh. 'I saved it, Fran. I saved my virginity for the man I loved.'

But he didn't love you back, Fran thought, flexing her hands on the table, unconsciously mirroring the movement of a fat, ginger cat who lay sprawled across one corner of the bar. 'And in spite of not loving you—he took the most precious thing you had to offer?'

'That's right,' sniffed Rosie. 'And I wasn't the only one!'

'You mean there were *others*?'

'Hundreds!'

'Hundreds?'

'Well, tens anyway. Loads!' Rosie spat the word out. 'Women who adored him. Women he didn't give tuppence for! Women who were all too easy to trick into his bed!'

'You're kidding!'

'I wish I was!'

Fran stared down at the silver gleam of the high-tech table, and thought of rich Sam Lockhart luring decent, hard-working girls like Rosie into his bed. A powerful man abusing that power to seduce innocent young women.

When she eventually lifted her golden-brown head to meet her friend's eyes, her own were deadly serious. She remembered the scrapes that Rosie had managed to land herself in at school, scrapes that Fran had somehow always got her out of. But this was different. Was it her place to help, even if she could?

'What do you want me to do?' she asked at last.

Rosie didn't even have to think about it. 'Nothing too major,' she shrugged. 'I'm not asking you to break any laws for me, Fran.'

'What then?'

'Just pay him back.'

CHAPTER TWO

FRAN'S fingers hovered uncertainly over the push-button telephone and she smiled at the irony of her situation. She was actually shaking. *Shaking.* She who was frightened of no man or no thing, was trembling like a schoolgirl at the thought of ringing Sam Lockhart.

Five minutes earlier she had already tapped the numbers out before hanging up immediately in a panic. Then thought how absolutely stupid *that* was! What if he had one of those sophisticated telephones which told him exactly who had called? He was probably used to lovesick women dialling the number and then changing their minds and hanging up. Did she want to arouse his suspicions by doing the same?

She punched the numbers out again, and listened to the ringing tone, certain that some minion would answer his mobile phone for him.

'Hel-lo?' The deep, velvety voice ringing down the line was as unexpected as it was irresistible. It *had* to be him—minions didn't sound like sex gods—and Fran had to frown with concentration to keep her voice steady.

'Sam Lockhart?' she said.

'Speaking.'

She drew a deep breath. 'Mr. Lockhart, you don't know me—'

'Not unless you decide to tell me your name, I don't,' he agreed softly.

Mistake number one. Ring someone up to try and

drum up their business, and then manage to sound as unprofessional as possible! 'It's Fran,' she said quickly. 'Fran Fisher.'

She could practically hear his mind flipping through its backlog of female names and coming up with a definite blank. But he was either too polite or too cautious to say so. Maybe he thought she was another in the long line of willing virgins offering herself up for pleasurable sacrifice!

'Are you a writer?' he asked in the wary and weary tone of someone who got more than their fair share of calls from would-be authors.

'No, I'm not.'

A sigh of relief. 'Thank God for that!' A note of caution returned to the deep voice. 'So what exactly can I do for you, Fran Fisher?'

'Actually, it's more a case of what I can do for you, Mr. Lockhart.'

'Oh?'

In that one word Fran heard resignation—as if he was gearing himself up to withstand a crude attempt at flirtation. Which, according to Rosie—was an occupational hazard when you happened to be Sam Lockhart.

And which meant there was nothing to be gained by playing for time. That would irritate a man like this, not intrigue him. She tried her most businesslike approach. 'Mr. Lockhart, I understand you're planning to hold a ball on Valentine's Day—'

'Are you a journalist?' he snapped.

'No, I'm not!'

'Who are you, then?'

'I told you—'

'I don't need you to tell me your name again! I've never met you before, have I?'

Well, it had taken him long enough to decide *that* and he still didn't sound one hundred per cent certain! She wondered how he would react if she adopted a sultry accent and purred, 'Are you sure?' 'No,' she said stiffly. 'You've never met me.'

'Yet you know the number of my mobile?'

She was tempted to mention that he was stating the obvious, but resisted. 'Yes.'

'How?'

'Er, your agency gave me the number.'

'Well, they shouldn't have!' he snapped. 'Certainly not to a complete stranger!' There was silence down the line for a moment. 'You've never met me and you're not a writer,' he mused. 'So what exactly *is* your angle, Fran Fisher?'

If it hadn't been for Rosie she probably would have hung up on him there and then. How absolutely ridiculous he sounded! Quizzing her as though she were some sort of second-rate spy and he the valuable prize within her sights! 'My "angle",' she said sweetly, 'is that I'm a professional party-planner—'

'But unsuccessful?' he suggested drawlingly.

'On the contrary!' she defended. 'I'm extremely successful!'

'So successful, in fact,' he continued, 'that you need to spend your time making cold calls to strangers in order to drum up a little business? I thought that your line of work relied solely on word-of-mouth recommendation?'

'Yes, of course it does! *Normally...*' She pulled a hideous face as she imagined him standing in the room with her. She *wanted* to dislike him, for Rosie's sake—and the way he was speaking to her meant that she didn't have to try very hard. But her dilemma lay in disliking him *too* much. Because if that happened, it would undoubtedly show in her attitude towards him, and then he certainly wouldn't give her the job! 'But I have to help things on their way. I've been working in Ireland, you see—'

He sounded weary. Like a man used to being bombarded with ambition. 'And now you want to break into the market over here?'

'Er…yes,' she stumbled, caught off guard. No need to tell him that this was going to be a one-off! 'Yes, I do. Actually, I'm quite well-known in Dublin. Ask anyone. And I've organised lots of fund-raisers—'

'Have you really?' he questioned, clearly not believing a word she said.

Fran bristled. 'I expect that if I mentioned some of my clients, their names would be instantly recognizable—even to you, Mr. Lockhart,' she told him stiffly.

'For example?' he shot back.

'I did some corporate work for the Irish Film Festival a couple of years ago, and on the back of that I got quite a few private functions. Cormack Casey, the screenwriter—he recommended me—'

'Cormack?' he interrupted, in surprise. 'You know him?'

'Well, not *intimately*,' she said, then wished she hadn't because it was obvious from the faint and disapproving intake of breath that he had misinterpreted her words. 'I organised the catering for the baptism of his first child.'

'Did you indeed?' asked Sam, in surprise. He'd been invited to that very same baptism, but a book tour in the States by one of his best-selling authors had put paid to that. 'And if I rang Cormack—he'd vouch for you, would he?'

'I certainly hope so. Triss—that's his wife—'

'I know who Triss is. I've known Cormack for years.'

'Oh. Well, she told me they'd be happy to help with references.' Fran suspected that the handsome Irish writer and his model wife had felt sorry for her. At the time she had been thinking about filing for a divorce from Sholto, and the baptism had been the only joyous thing in her life. She had poured her heart and soul into making the party match the moving ceremony of baptism, and she had been inundated with work ever since....

'Did she?' Sam Lockhart sounded impressed.

Fran cleared her throat, sensing that this was just the right time to appeal to his greed. 'The thing is, Mr. Lockhart—if you hire me to organise your ball for you, then I guarantee we will raise more money than you ever dreamed of.'

'That's fighting talk,' Sam commented drily, then added, 'Who told you about it, by the way?'

'You mean the ball?'

'No, Man landing on the moon!' he drawled sarcastically. 'Yes, of course I mean the ball!'

This might have been tricky if she hadn't anticipated the question. But Rosie had said that he was vain enough and realistic enough to know that everyone in his circle and beyond, would be clamouring for an invitation.

'Oh, no one in particular,' she said vaguely. 'You know what it's like. People talk. Particularly before an event has been organised—it gives them a certain cachet if they know about a highly desirable party before it's officially been advertised.' She drew a deep breath and added shamelessly, 'And believe me, Mr. Lockhart— from what I understand—this is going to be the hottest ticket in town.'

'I hope so,' he said thoughtfully. 'Well, I already have someone in mind for the job, I'm afraid. Several women have already offered—'

She could imagine! 'Amateurs?' asked Fran sharply. 'Or professionals?'

'Well, all of them have organised similar functions before—'

'You know exactly where you are with a professional,' put in Fran smoothly.

'Really?' He sounded unconvinced.

It was time for a little feminine desperation. To see whether a breathy, heartfelt plea would get through to the man Rosie had described as a 'virile robot.' 'Won't you at least *see* me, Mr. Lockhart?' she questioned.

'I'm a busy man.'

'Well, of course you are!' She used the soothing tone of a children's nanny, then added a little flattery for good measure. 'Successful men always are. But could you forgive yourself if your hectic schedule meant that your ball didn't fulfill all your expectations, simply because you wouldn't make time to see me?'

He actually laughed at this—a bubbling, honeyed chuckle—and it was such a warm and sexy sound that Fran found herself gripping the receiver as though it might fly out of her fingers.

'Determination is a quality I admire almost as much as self-belief,' he mused. 'Provided it is backed up by talent—'

'Oh, it is!'

There was a pause. 'Very well, Miss Fisher—I'll give you exactly ten minutes to convince me that I'd be a fool not to employ you.'

Thank God! 'You won't regret it, Mr. Lockhart,' she enthused, hoping that her voice carried no trace of insincerity. 'Tell me where and tell me when and I'll be there!'

'Okay. How about this afternoon?'

'You mean *today*?'

'Well, I certainly don't mean tomorrow,' he purred. 'I'm flying to Europe with one of my authors later on this evening. I can see you at home—briefly—before I leave.'

He managed to make it sound as though he was making an appointment for her at the dentist—and come to think of it, her adrenalin levels were as high as they might have been if he *were* a dentist! 'In London?' she guessed hopefully, since Rosie had already informed her that he had a flat in town and a house somewhere in the country.

'No, in Cambridge,' he stated.

'Cambridge,' she repeated faintly, her heart sinking as she thought of travelling to the flat, ploughed fields of the fens on a filthy cold November afternoon. Maybe on a fool's mission.

'Is getting to Cambridge going to be a problem for you, Miss Fisher?' he questioned. 'It's hardly on the other side of the world, you know!'

Rule number one: a party-planner must be prepared for any eventuality! 'Problem? None whatsoever!' she lied cheerfully. 'Just give me a few easy-to-understand directions and I'll be there in time for tea!'

'I can hardly wait,' he said, and Fran could have sworn that he was *laughing* at her.

The light was already fading from the sky when the train pulled into Eversford station and the bleak, unwelcoming platform made Fran feel as though she was on the film-set of an old-fashioned murder mystery.

She knotted her scarf tightly around her neck and looked around. Sam Lockhart had told her where she could get a cab and she walked out of the station into the dreary afternoon, where a fine mist of grey rain clogged the air and slicked onto the roofs of the cars like grease.

There was no one else in the queue and the driver looked at her with interest as she told him the name of the house.

'Sam Lockhart's place,' he commented, as he switched on his meter and pulled out of the station fore-court.

'You know it?'

'Should do. He brings us plenty of work. Thought that's where you'd be headed,' he said, smiling.

Fran, who was hunting around in her handbag for a mirror, paused, mid-search. 'Oh?' She smiled back. 'Can you guess where all your passengers are headed, then?'

'No. Just his.' The driver stopped at some red lights and grinned at her in his rear mirror. 'If it's someone glamorous getting off the London train, then the odds are that she wants to go out to Sam Lockhart's place!'

Fran bristled as the driver's giveaway remark reminded her why she was here in the first place. Poor Rosie! 'Oh?' She thought how indignant she sounded! 'He has a whole stream of women arriving here, does he?'

The driver shook his head hastily. 'Oh, no! Never more than one at a time!' he joked. 'And we only notice because nothing much happens around here. It's a pretty isolated place.'

'So I see.' Fran looked out of the window as the buildings and lights of the town began to get more sparse and the landscape began to acquire the vast, untouched emp-

tiness of perfectly flat countryside. It could have been
boring, but she thought that it had a stark, distinctive
beauty all of its own. Even so, its very bleakness did not
fit in with her idea of where a sex god would live. Why
had he chosen to settle out here, she wondered, when he
could be raving it up in London? 'Is it very far?'

'Another couple of miles,' he answered, slowing the
car right down as the lane narrowed. 'Writer, are you?'

'Not me, I'm afraid!' she told him cheerfully, and
picked up her hand mirror to see what sort of face Sam
Lockhart would be greeted by.

Unexciting was the word which immediately sprang
to mind.

Her skin looked too pale, but then it always did—and
the green-gold eyes could have done with a little more
mascara to make the best of them. But apart from the
fact that she had left in a hurry, Fran had deliberately
played safe, unwilling to look as though she'd spent
hours in front of the mirror in an effort to impress Sam
Lockhart. Apart from the fact that it just wasn't her
style—sex gods were used to women slapping on the
entire contents of their make-up bags. She knew that
from living with her husband. So she would be different.
Because there was one other thing she knew about that
particular breed of man...they were easily bored and
something different always intrigued them.

So she had contented herself with a slick of nude lip-
stick which simply looked like she had been licking her
lips. Just enough make-up to look as though she wasn't
wearing any at all—but only a woman would be able to
tell that!

'Here we are!' said the driver. The car slowed down
and began indicating right as a high, dark hedge began
to loom up beside them. Before her stretched a long

drive which curved off unexpectedly to the left, and impulse made her lean over to tap the driver on the shoulder.

'Would you mind stopping here?' she asked.

'It's a long drive.'

'I can see that. I don't mind walking. In fact I'd rather walk. I just want to get the...*feel*...of the place first.' That first gut reaction to someone's home was invaluable. Houses and owners taken unawares told you volumes about what they were *really* like—and the better you knew a client, the better you would be able to judge the perfect party for their particular needs. A car drawing up outside would alert Sam Lockhart to her arrival and that would not do. She wanted to see the face of the seducer taken off guard.

Ignoring the driver's curious expression, she paid her fare and gave him a healthy tip.

'Thanks very much, Miss. Will you be wanting to go back to the station...tonight?' He put the question so delicately that Fran might have laughed if she weren't feeling so indignant on Rosie's behalf. What was Lockhart running here, for goodness' sake? A harem?

'Yes, I will,' she answered crisply. 'But I don't know what time that will be—so if you'd give me one of your cards I'll ring.'

She waited until the red tail-lights of the car had retreated before setting off up the wide path, her sensible brown leather boots sending little shoals of gravel spraying in her wake.

The grounds—they were much too extensive to be called a garden—wore the muddy, leafless brown of a winter coat, but the sparse flower-beds were curved and beautifully shaped, and the trees had been imaginatively planted to stand dramatically against the huge, bare sky.

The house was old. A beautifully proportioned white-washed villa which was perfect in its simplicity.

And it looked deserted.

Moving quietly, Fran crept forward to peer into one of the leaded windows at the front of the house, and nearly died with shock when she saw a man sitting in there, before the golden flicker of a log fire. A dark, denim-clad figure sprawled in a comfortable-looking armchair, his long legs stretched in front of him as he read from what looked like a manuscript.

She came to within nose-pressing distance of the window and her movement must have caught his attention, for he looked up from his reading and his dark-featured face registered no emotion whatsoever at seeing her standing there. Not surprise or fright or irritation. Not even a mild curiosity.

Then he pointed a rather dismissive finger in the direction of the front of the house and mimed, 'the door's open.'

And started reading again!

How very *rude*, she thought! Especially when she'd travelled all this way to see him! Fran crunched her way over to the front door, pushed it open and stepped inside, narrowing her eyes with surprise as she looked around.

It wasn't what she had expected.

On the wooden floor lay mud-covered wellington boots, a gardening catalogue, a pair of secateurs and a battered old panama hat. Waterproof coats and jackets were heaped on the coat stand and a variety of different coloured umbrellas stood in an untidy stack behind the front door. The walls were deep and scarlet and womb-like and welcoming.

So where were the wall-to-wall mirrors and the

shaggy fur rugs where he made lots of love to lots of different women?

It felt like coming home, she thought, with an unwelcome jolt. And it *shouldn't*, she told herself fiercely. This was the house of the man who was responsible for Rosie's heartache—not the house of her dreams!

She turned and walked along a narrow corridor which led to the study and stood framed in the doorway with the light behind her.

He looked up, all unshaven and ruffled, as if he'd just got out of bed. Or hadn't been to bed. 'Hi,' he said, and yawned. 'You must be Fran Fisher.'

His eyes were the most incredible shade of deep blue, she noticed—night-dark and piercing and remarkable enough to eclipse even the rugged symmetry of his face. With the jeans went untidy, slightly too-long hair, making him more rock-star than literary agent.

Yes, Fran thought, her heart pounding like a mad thing. No wonder Rosie had fallen so badly. He looked *exactly* like a sex god! 'And you must be Sam Lockhart,' she gulped.

He shot a brief glance at his wristwatch and she found herself thinking that she had never seen a man so at ease in his own skin as this one.

'Yeah,' he drawled. 'That's me!'

'Nice of you to come to the door and meet me!'

'If you can't manage to navigate your way from the front door to the study, then I think you're in the wrong job, honey.' He yawned again. 'Come in and sit down.'

Fran gazed around the room. 'Where?'

Sam conceded that she did have a point. Just about every available surface was given over to manuscripts of varying thicknesses. Some had even overflowed from his desk to form small paper towers on the Persian rug.

'Don't you ever clear up after you?' she asked, before she had time to think about whether or not it was a wise question.

'If you tidy manuscripts away, you lose them,' he shrugged, as he rescued the telephone from underneath a shoal of papers. 'At least if they're staring you in the face you can't hide away from the fact that you need to get around to reading them sometime!'

The blue eyes glanced rather absently around the study. 'Though maybe it *is* a little cluttered in here. The sitting room is just along there.' He pointed towards a low door at the far end of the room. 'Why don't you trot along and wait for me in there. Make yourself comfortable. I'm expecting a call any minute, but I shan't be long.'

'Please don't rush on my account,' she gritted, irritated at being told to trot along—as if she was some kind of pit-pony!

This drew a sardonic smile. 'Don't worry, I won't.'

The first thing Fran decided when she walked into Sam Lockhart's sitting room, was that there was no woman living in the house with him—or if there was, then she must be a very passive and insipid woman because the place had masculinity stamped indelibly all over it. Deep, bold colours and substantial furniture.

Fran was used to being in strangers' houses; it was part of her job. She knew how much a home environment could tell you about a person, and over the years she had become an expert at reading the signs of domestic bliss.

Or turmoil.

The room had all the untidy informality of truly bachelor territory. For a start he seemed to be incapable of throwing away a single newspaper—since she could see

Sunday supplements dating back from the previous month, and beyond. And there were enough books heaped on a low table and on the floor surrounding it for him to consider opening his own personal library! She crouched briefly to scan some of the titles and was alarmed to see that they shared some of the same taste in authors. Disturbing.

She rose to her feet and carried on looking. There were no photos scattered anywhere, but that didn't really surprise her. Women were the ones who put photos in a room—reminders of great family occasions like engagements and weddings and christenings. Which were also a mark of possession and ownership—marks that men seemed to need less than woman.

She picked up a beautifully worked tapestry cushion which was lying on the chair, and was so busy examining it that she didn't hear him come into the room. It was only when she turned around to find herself being studied intently by a pair of dark-blue eyes that Fran realised he was standing watching her.

Still holding onto the cushion, she blinked. As well as taking the phone call, he must have washed his face and swiftly shaved the blue-black blur of shadow away from the square chin. And run a comb through the dark tangle of his hair. He had put a dark sweater on too, and the soft navy cashmere clung to the definition of broad shoulders.

Suddenly, his blue eyes looked even bluer, so that their soft brilliance seemed to cut right through you, like a sword. Oh, my goodness, she thought weakly, he really *is* gorgeous. Fran clutched the cushion against her chest, like a breastplate, and saw him frown.

'Planning to take that home with you?' he queried softly.

Fran stared down at the cushion in her hands. On one side the single word Sam was embroidered, in a heart-shaped frame made of tiny scarlet flowers. On the other side was an intricately crafted message which said, A love given can never be taken away.

'This is beautiful,' she said politely, wondering who the maker of the cushion was. Someone who obviously adored him. 'Absolutely beautiful.'

So why did his face close up so that it looked all shuttered and cold?

'Yes,' he said repressively. 'It is.'

Part of her job was asking questions; making connections. If she saw something she liked she tried to find out where it came from, because you never knew when you might want one just like it. 'Do you mind me asking where you got it from?'

His eyes narrowed and Fran was surprised by the sudden appearance of pain which briefly hardened their appearance from blue to bruise. So he could be hurt, could he?

'Yes, I do mind! I told you that I had a plane to catch,' he said coldly. 'Yet you seem to want to spend what little time we have discussing soft furnishings.'

Feeling slightly fazed at the criticism, Fran quickly put the cushion back down on the sofa and looked at him expectantly. 'Sorry about that,' she said lightly. 'Force of habit.'

He didn't even acknowledge the apology. 'Why don't we just get down to business.'

Standing there, with her sheepskin coat making her feel distinctly overdressed, Fran felt hot and out-of-place and very slightly foolish. He could have done with a crash course in common courtesy, she thought. 'Mind if I take my coat off first?'

'Feel free.'

She noticed that he didn't attempt to help her remove the heavy, fur-lined garment and was irritated with herself for even caring. He was a future client—hopefully—not somebody she would be taking home to meet her mother!

She draped the coat over the arm of a chair and stood in front of him, feeling slightly awkward, and not in the least bit confident. So now what did she do? She found herself wondering what was going on behind those dark eyes of his. And what he saw when he looked at her in that curiously intent way of his.

Her clothes were practical and comfortable, in that order—it went with the job. Very short skirts which meant you couldn't bend over without inhibition were out. So were spindly and unsafe heels designed to make legs look longer. But although Fran was a little curvier than she would have ideally liked, she was also tall enough to carry off most clothes with style. Today, her brown woollen skirt skimmed her leather-booted ankles and the warm, cream sweater cleverly concealed the thermal vest which lay beneath.

She glanced at him to see if there was any kind of reaction to her appearance, but Sam Lockhart's expression remained as enigmatic as the Mona Lisa. Now why did that bother her? Because the arch-philanderer didn't think she warranted a second look? For heaven's sake, woman, she told herself—you're here to avenge some broken hearts—not join their ranks!

'So are you going to sit down?' he murmured. 'I'd prefer to stretch my legs before my flight, but there's no reason why the interview should be uncomfortable for you, is there?'

'Er, no, I'll stay standing,' she stumbled. 'W-what interview?'

'The interview which helps me decide whether to give you the job or not.' A mocking look. 'What else did you think this was going to be? A tea party? I have to decide whether I want you to work for me and you have to decide whether or not you could bear to.' Another mocking look. 'Or did you think the job would be yours the moment I stared into those great big golden-green eyes of yours?'

Fran blinked with astonishment. So, beneath that cool exterior he *had* been noticing the way she looked! 'No, of course I didn't!' she retorted, feeling slightly reassured that he had started to flirt with her. It kind of reinforced what Rosie had told her to expect. 'I'm a professional through and through and I'd *never* use sex appeal to sell myself!'

'Not consciously, perhaps?' he challenged softly. 'But most women use their sex quite ruthlessly—in my experience.'

'And that's extensive, is it?' she challenged in return.

'That depends on your definition of extensive,' came the silky reply. 'But I would advise against making assumptions like that about a man you've only just met.'

There was nothing to be gained by irritating him, and clearly she *was* irritating him. Very much. 'Sorry,' she backtracked hastily.

'So can I see your portfolio?' he asked.

'My...portfolio?'

'You do *have* a portfolio showing me examples of your work?'

'Of course I do,' she said. She just hadn't been planning on using it... 'But unfortunately I had to leave it with a client in Ireland. Anyway, word-of-mouth is the best recommendation—and the only way you can assess my work is to speak to some of the people who've hired me in the past.'

'I already did.'

She shouldn't have been surprised. But she was. 'Who?'

'Cormack Casey. His was the only name you gave me. Fortunately he's the kind of man I trust.'

Fran blinked. On the phone he had said that he knew Cormack, but the warmth in his voice suggested a deeper relationship than mere acquaintanceship. 'You mean you're friends?'

'Yes, we are. What's the matter?' He raised his eyebrows. 'You sound surprised?'

Well, she was. Because Cormack, for all his good looks and sex appeal, was fiercely loyal to his wife, Triss. A one-woman man. A man with morals. So how come he was matey with the arch-heartbreaker Sam Lockhart?

'What did Cormack tell you about me?'

'That you were good.' There was a pause. 'Very good.'

'Now *you* sound surprised!' she observed.

He shrugged. 'People who are good don't usually have to go out looking for business. Not in your line of work. Cormack was a little taken aback when I told him you'd rung me. In fact, he found it difficult to believe.'

Fran felt the first prickle of apprehension. 'D-did he?'

'Mmmm. He said it was completely out of character. Said you were cool and sought-after and he couldn't imagine *you* ever *touting for trade*.' He emphasised the words with a brief, black-hearted smile.

It was an offensive way to put it and Fran prayed that she wouldn't start blushing. And not to be disconcerted by the intense question in those blue eyes. Maybe not looking at him was the only way to guarantee that.

'So why start now?' he mused.

'Well, I've been working in Ireland,' she defended, swallowing down her anxiety. 'No one knows me here in England—and I needed to do something. Something big to get me established over here.'

'And working for me will do that?'

She met his gaze reluctantly, feeling the erratic pumping of her heart in response. Did he have this effect on anyone with two X chromosomes in their body, she wondered? 'You know it will,' she answered bluntly.

There was a brief hooding of his eyes as he nodded, as if acknowledging her honesty. If only he knew, Fran thought, with the slightest shimmer of guilt. Until she remembered Rosie's tear-stained face. And her damning list of just how many hearts he had broken along the way. Sam Lockhart deserved everything he was about to get! That is, if she got the job....

'So my Valentine ball will put you firmly on the map?' he observed.

Fran nodded.

'That's what I can do for you,' he mused, and his voice was a soft caress which whispered temptingly at her senses. 'Which leaves me wondering what I'll get from you in return?'

It was blatant. Flagrant. Outrageous. Fran's hand hovered above and then clutched onto her pearl necklace, her fingers sliding over the slippery surface of the lustrous jewels. Rosie had said he was rampant—but she had been expecting a little more finesse than *that*. '*W-what* exactly did you have in mind?' she demanded hoarsely.

He frowned, and his gaze seemed to scorch her skin

as he searched her face. He seemed to be keeping a straight face with some difficulty as he observed her reaction. 'This is purely a business transaction, Miss Fisher,' he reminded her wryly. 'Not a sexual one.'

Fran's face went scarlet. 'I wasn't suggesting for a moment—'

'Oh, yes, you were,' he contradicted softly. 'It was written all over your face. And your body.' His voice lowered. 'I'm flattered.'

'Well, don't be!' she snapped. 'Maybe I *did* jump to the wrong conclusion, but women have to be on their guard against innuendo. Against men coming on strong.'

'Yes, I can imagine that you must keep coming up against that kind of thing,' he commented innocently.

Fran looked at him suspiciously. Was he making fun of her? 'Perhaps we should talk about the ball now,' she said primly.

He gave a wolfish smile, aware that he was finding this verbal skirmish *extremely stimulating* indeed. 'But that's exactly what I've been trying to do for the last five minutes. You *do* dither, don't you, Miss Fisher?'

'Not normally, no—it must be the effect you're having on me!' Fran took a deep breath as she forced herself to ignore his sarcasm and to inject her voice with enthusiasm. 'Anyway, Valentine's Day is such a *fantastic* date for any kind of party!' she began breezily. 'It gives us so much *scope* for decorations!'

'Such as?'

'Oh, you know.... Hearts! Flowers! Love! Romance!'

'Aren't you forgetting originality?' he put in, his face deadpan.

Now he *was* making fun of her. Fran frowned, forgetting Rosie, forgetting everything except doing what she was good at. And she was very good at pitching for a job....'Mr. Lockhart—' She gave him a patient look. 'Valentine's Day is just like Christmas—'

'It is?'

'It certainly is. As a traditional celebration—people expect certain customs to be adhered to.'

'They do?'

'Of course they do!' she enthused, really warming to her subject now. 'Its rituals comfort and reassure—because people don't always want to be surprised, you know. They want the predictable—'

'How very boring,' he murmured.

Fran cleared her throat. That sizzling little glance of his was annoyingly distracting. 'Wrong!' she smiled. 'I can assure you that while what I am suggesting may not exactly be ground-breaking stuff—'

'Mmmm?'

'It most certainly will not be *boring*! You will have the very best food and wines and the most wonderful music—all served up in a setting which will quite simply take your breath away!'

His eyes rested on her thoughtfully for a moment or two, before shooting another glance at his watch. 'Right. Well, thank you very much for your time, Miss Fisher.'

Fran stared at him in astonishment. Surely that wasn't *it*? Yes, he'd said ten minutes, but he'd barely let her talk for more than thirty seconds! She glanced at her own watch. No. A man of his word. It had been ten minutes exactly. 'You mean, that's it?'

'I'm afraid so. You see, it really *is* time that I was leaving for the airport. I can drop you off at the station on the way if you like.'

The words were as dismissive as the way he said them. So that was that. No job. No pay-back. She'd let Rosie down, but even worse, she'd let herself down, by stupidly jumping to the conclusion that he had been coming on to her. That was why he wasn't going to give her the job. Acting naive and gauche round a man like this, as though she was still wet around the ears. Instead of a woman who had single-handedly built up a thriving business for herself out of the ruins of her failed marriage.

'No, I'll take a cab.'

'Sure? It'll be quicker by car.' The lazy smile grew wider. 'Or don't you trust yourself to be alone in the car with me?'

Huh! She might be leaving without the job. She might have travelled halfway across the country on one of the filthiest days of the year. But there was no need for her to leave with him thinking that she was some kind of emotional *hysteric*. She had underestimated Sam Lockhart and her rather dizzy reaction to him, and for that she had paid the price. It was time to withdraw in a cool and dignified manner.

'Don't be absurd, Mr. Lockhart,' she said, forcing a cool smile. 'I'd love a lift. Just as long as it isn't out of your way?'

'No, not at all. Come on.'

He paused only to pick up a compact-looking brief-case in the hall and to engage in a complex locking-system for the front door. 'The car's out in the garage at the back,' he said.

His long legs covered the ground at twice the pace she was used to, but she managed to keep up with him on their way to the stable-block which had been converted to house a clutch of cars. But Sam Lockhart was obviously not a man who collected wealthy toys—for there was only one vehicle sitting there. Fran had expected something predictable—the rich man's phallic

substitute of a long, low car in screaming scarlet or dev-
ilish black.

Instead she saw a mud-splattered four-wheel drive
which had golf clubs and a tennis racket companionably
jumbled around a tartan picnic rug in the back, along
with a muddle of magazines and discarded sweet wrap-
pers. An empty water bottle lay next to a pair of battered
old running shoes. A large brown envelope marked
Sam—*Urgent!* lay on the passenger seat.

This was the car of an action-packed life, whose
owner had neither the time nor the inclination to vacuum
the carpet, thought Fran. It did *not* look like the car of
a playboy, she thought with mild confusion.

He saw her expression of surprise. 'Excuse the state
of the car.'

'No, I like it,' she said, without thinking. 'Honestly.
It's homely.'

He smiled. 'Mmmm. Messy might be more accurate,'
he murmured. He moved the envelope, threw his suitcase
in the back and waited until Fran had strapped herself
in before starting the engine.

His driving surprised her, too. That did not fit with
the rich-man stereotype, either. No roar of accelerator or
screech of brakes. His driving was safe, not showy—just
like the car. Bizarrely, Fran even felt herself relaxing,
until she reminded herself just who was next to her, and
sat bolt upright to stare fixedly out of the window.

But he didn't seem to notice her frozen posture, just
switched on the radio and listened to the news channel.
He didn't speak during the entire journey to the station
and neither did Fran. She couldn't think of a thing to
say. Well, she could. But something simpered on the
lines of, 'I hope you didn't get the wrong idea about me
earlier' would damn her even further in his eyes, and

she wasn't prepared to do that. Not even for Rosie. But more especially for herself. Because for some unfathomable reason, she would rather have made a fool of herself in front of anyone than in front of Sam Lockhart.

She was desperate for the journey to end, yet her heart sank with disappointment as the car bumped across the station forecourt. I won't ever see him again, she thought, wondering why it should matter.

'Thanks for the lift.' She owed him the brief glance, the polite smile, but was totally unprepared for the watchfulness in his blue eyes.

'I don't have your card,' he said.

'My card?' she repeated stupidly.

'Your business card.'

She scarcely dared hope why he wanted it, just fumbled around in her handbag until she found one. 'Here.'

He glanced at it. 'This is a Dublin code.'

'Well, there's my mobile number,' she pointed. 'You can always reach me on that.'

'When are you going back to Ireland?'

'I'm…not sure.' She hadn't decided, because her decision was based on whether he gave her the job or not. Somehow she doubted it—but she certainly wouldn't find out by trying to read his mind. She tried not to sound either too nervous or too tentative. 'Am I still in the running for the job, then?'

'No.' There was a pause as the word dropped like a guillotine, severing all her hopes. Poor Rosie, she thought fleetingly, until she realised that he was speaking again, but so quietly that she had to strain her ears to hear.

'The job is yours.'

'Pardon?'

'The job is yours,' he repeated, eyes gleaming as he

enjoyed her startled reaction. 'That is, if you still want it?'

'Er, yes. I still want it,' she answered, wondering why victory—and such unexpected victory—should taste so hollow. But she had to know. 'But why? I mean, why are you offering it to me?'

He frowned. 'I wouldn't have thought that it was particularly good psychology to sound so incredulous if someone offers you the job.' His eyes narrowed critically. 'It might even make *some* people reconsider.'

'Well, I certainly didn't give the best interview of my life,' she told him candidly.

'No, you didn't,' he agreed. 'But Cormack said you were the best—'

She gave a slow flush of pleasure. 'Did he?'

'Yeah, he did. And he's the kind of man whose opinion people listen to—me included.'

'And that's why you're offering me the job—because of Cormack's say-so?'

'Partly. But also because you're a fresh face on the scene, and fresh faces bring enthusiasm. I've never hosted a ball before, and I want it to work.' His blue eyes gleamed with a hard determination. 'Really work.'

Suddenly all her old fervour was back. The ball *would* be a success. She would make sure of that. Rosie's payback was merely an offshoot—an insignificant little offshoot. A lesson he needed to learn which would probably benefit him in the end! And who knew, maybe one day he might even be grateful to her! 'Oh, it'll work, all right—I can guarantee you that, Mr. Lockhart,' she breathed.

'Sam,' he corrected.

'Sam,' Fran repeated obediently. It felt so right to say

his name. Too right. Like having one long lean leg mere inches away from hers felt right, too.

Not since Sholto had she been so tuned in to a man's presence. Only this seemed all wrong. This wasn't just a knockout individual with searing blue eyes and a body which had been constructed in the dream-factory. This was the man who had robbed her best friend of her innocence.

So why did she find herself wanting to curl up like a kitten in his lap, instead of lashing out at him with her claws?

'I'll be out of the country all week,' he told her. 'I'll ring you when I get back and we'll arrange a meet in London to discuss details and budget, that kind of thing. Okay with you?'

'Sure,' she nodded, and was just reaching over to unlock the car door when he suddenly leaned over and caught hold of her left hand and turned it over to study it closely.

'No marks, I see,' he observed, tracing her bare ring finger with the pad of his thumb.

All she could feel was the rough warmth of his skin and the shock of the unexpected contact made every sane thought trickle out of her mind. 'I b-beg your pardon?'

'Marks. From your wedding ring.'

'Who told you I was married? Cormack?'

The blaze from his eyes was like a searchlight. 'Yeah. Who else? You don't wear the fact tattooed on your forehead, that's for sure!'

Fran shifted awkwardly on her seat. 'Well, that's past tense. I'm divorced now.'

'So I understand. There's a lot of it around,' he drawled. 'But even so...' He let his thumb trickle slowly around the base of her finger in a gesture which to Fran seemed both highly suggestive and highly erotic and she shivered despite the warmth of the car. 'Wedding rings always leave their mark—one way or the other.'

This was getting too close for comfort. Fran tore her hand away from his and pushed open the car door, her breath coming hot and thick in her throat. 'I'll see you when you get back from Europe,' she croaked.

CHAPTER THREE

FRAN rang the doorbell and moments later a blurry-eyed Rosie peered out from behind the safety chain.

'Wassa time?' she mumbled.

Fran frowned and stared at her friend in horror and amazement. 'Five o'clock. Rosie, have you been drinking?'

Rosie swallowed back a hiccup and then beamed. 'I jus'…jus' ha' a small one. I was nervous, see. Knowing that you were meeting Sam.' Her eyes focussed at last. 'Did you? Meet him?'

'I did.'

'And?'

Fran shivered. It had been a long and boring journey back on the train which had stopped at about a hundred stations between Eversford and London. She was cold and she was tired and frankly, not at all sure that she was doing the right thing in trying to teach Rosie's ex-lover a lesson. From her brief meeting with him, he had not seemed the ideal candidate to have the wool pulled over his eyes. She was going to have to be very careful....

'Rosie, do we have to *have* this conversation on the doorstep?'

'Oh! Sorry! Come in!' Rosie unhooked the chain and Fran followed her into the flat which seemed to have had nothing done to it in the way of housework since she had been there the day before yesterday. She wrinkled her nose. How *stale* it smelt.

Rosie turned to her eagerly. 'So! Did you get the job?'

Again, Fran felt the oddest shiver of apprehension. 'Yes, I did.'

'Oh, joy of joys!' gurgled Rosie. 'Well done! Let's go and have a drink to celebrate!'

'Haven't you had enough?'

Rosie looked at her sharply. 'Maybe I have,' she shrugged. 'But that doesn't stop you, does it?'

'No, I'm fine. I had tea on the train. I just want to take the weight off my feet.'

Fran waited until they were both settled in the sitting room where dirty cups and glasses littered the coffee table, before she said anything.

'The place could do with a bit of a clean-up, you know, Rosie.'

Rosie pulled a face. 'Bet you didn't say that to Sam! He's nearly as untidy as me! God, I used to despair of the way he dropped his shirts on the bedroom floor!'

It was a statement which told how intimate they had been, and Fran clenched her teeth as she tried to block out the image of Sam Lockhart peeling the clothes from that impressive body of his. Surely she wasn't *jealous*? Not of Rosie? But maybe it was that which made her plump for a home truth rather than sparing Rosie's feelings any longer. 'He may be untidy,' she agreed sternly. 'But at least his house is clean.'

Rosie, who was in the process of rubbing her finger at a sticky brown ring left by a sherry glass, looked up abruptly. 'Are you saying my flat is dirty?'

'I'm saying it could do with an airing,' said Fran diplomatically. 'And a bit of a blitz.'

Rosie nodded with the distracted air of someone who wasn't really listening. 'Tell me what Sam said first. Tell me what you thought of him.'

Fran chose her next words even more carefully. 'He's certainly very good-looking. I can see why you fell for him.'

Rosie squinted. 'C'mon, Fran. You can do better than that. What did you *really* think of him?'

Tricky. 'Well, he wasn't what I was expecting,' she said slowly.

'Mmmm? What were you expecting then?'

Fran wriggled her shoulders as she tried to put it into words. 'The way you described him, I thought he'd be kind of...*obvious*. You know. Mr. Smarm. But he wasn't. He was...' Now she really couldn't go on. Being honest was one thing, but not if it had the effect of wounding the very person you were supposed to be helping. And if Fran told Rosie the truth—that she had been more attracted to him than any man since Sholto—then wouldn't that make *her* look foolish? And an appalling judge of character?

'Sexy?' enquired Rosie.

Fran winced. It would not have been her first word of choice. 'I suppose so.'

'That's because he is. Very. Fran, I didn't have any real experience of men before I met Sam—but believe me when I tell you that he is just *dynamite* in bed—'

'Rosie! I don't want to know!'

'Why not?'

'Because other people's sex lives should remain private, that's why!' Except that she wasn't being completely truthful. It was more that she couldn't *bear* to think of Sam Lockhart being intimate with anyone—and the reasons for that were confusing the hell out of her. 'Change the subject, Rosie!' she growled. 'Or I'll wash my hands of the whole idea!'

'Okay, okay—keep your hair on!' Rosie slanted her a

glance from beneath the heavy fringe which flopped into her eyes. 'So what's happening about the ball?'

'He's ringing me when he gets back from Europe. That's when we'll discuss all the details. You know, the budget, the venue—' she yawned. 'That kind of thing.'

'And the guest list?'

'That's right. Most of the planning I can organise by phone from Dublin, but I'm going to need a temporary base in London.'

'Stay here with me!' said Rosie impulsively.

Fran shook her head. She suspected that a few years down the line, sharing a flat might test their friendship to breaking point. 'How can I, Rosie?' she asked gently. '*You* live here. And Sam knows you live here, doesn't he? I know it's unlikely, but imagine if he saw me coming out of your flat. It would rather give the game away, wouldn't it? No, I'll ring my mother up—she's got loads of rich friends and relatives. One of them might just be planning a winter holiday in the sun. I could do with a few weeks off—and I'm the world's best house-sitter!'

She studied the finger that Sam had so softly circled, and swallowed. 'You know, maybe this is the opportunity I need to make the break and get out of Ireland—'

'I thought you loved it!'

'I do. Just that Dublin is such a small city—'

'And you keep running into Sholto and his new girl-friend, I suppose?'

Fran forced a smile. 'Something like that.' She stood up decisively. 'Got any bleach?'

'*Bleach?*' Rosie blinked. 'You aren't planning to go blond, are you?' she asked in horror.

Fran's smile widened of its own accord. 'Not *that* kind

of bleach, stupid! I meant the kind that cleans floors!'

'Oh, *that*!' said Rosie gloomily, and went off to find some.

By the time Sam Lockhart rang her a week later, Fran had established a London base she could use whenever she needed. One of her mother's many cousins was visiting her daughter in Australia for the winter, leaving a high-ceilinged flat vacant in Hampstead village—in a road which was apparently a burglar's paradise.

'She'd be delighted to have you keeping your eye on the place,' Fran's mother had said. 'But I'd like to see you myself, darling. When are you coming up to Scotland?'

Fran prodded a neglected-looking plant which was badly in need of a gallon or two of water, and frowned. 'I promise I'll be there for Christmas.'

'What—not until then?'

'Mum, it's only weeks away.' Fran kept her voice patient.

'Is Rosie any better?'

'A bit. Still misses this man Sam Lockhart.'

'Didn't that all finish ages ago?'

'Uh-huh. I guess some broken hearts just take longer to heal than others.' But Fran deliberately omitted to mention the fact that Sam was one of her new clients. The information would be bound to set her mother thinking, and for some strange reason Fran was convinced that she would try to talk her out of getting involved in some kind of vendetta.

There was a long and loaded pause followed by a question which was studiedly casual. 'So how's Sholto?'

The pause from Fran's end was equally loaded. 'How should I know, Mum? I don't have anything to do with

Sholto anymore. Why would I, when we're divorced now? Apparently, he's got a new girlfriend—'

'Well, *that* doesn't surprise me—'

'Er, yes. Listen, Mum, I have to go now.' And Fran abruptly ended the conversation.

It was funny. When people heard that you were divorcing, or divorced, they always asked whether you had any children. And when Fran said that no, they didn't, the response was always the same. 'Oh, *that's* all right, then.' As though a marriage didn't matter if there weren't any offspring involved.

But it *did* matter. Divorce left a stubborn stain behind which you could never quite shift. And it affected people's attitudes towards you. Fran could read it in her mother's disappointed voice. She had read it the other day in Sam's rather disdainful reaction. What had he said? 'There's a lot of it around.' As though it was some kind of nasty infectious disease! And he was right. The world was full of divorced people, and however amicable the agreement, it marked you out like a leper....

Fran's mobile phone shrilled into life early one morning, exactly a week after Sam Lockhart had dropped her off at the train station.

The deep voice was instantly recognizable—it was just that Fran, emerging from a restless night's sleep, was not at her sharpest. She had spent the previous evening at the cinema with Rosie, who had insisted they leave halfway through the film, because apparently the leading actor in it had reminded her of Sam. Fran hadn't been able to see it herself. True, he had Sam's startling blue eyes, but not their intensity, and the face had been much softer....

So the two of them had gone to eat an indulgent supper instead, which had ended up with Rosie drinking far too much and sobbing into her bread and butter pudding that her life was a vacuum, and it was all Sam's fault. Listening to a different version of the same story Fran felt as though she was on a fast train to nowhere....

Fran opened bleary eyes and picked up the phone. 'Hel-lo?' she yawned sleepily.

'It's Sam Lockhart.'

She sat bolt upright in bed. 'Oh, my goodness!'

'Sam Lockhart,' he repeated impatiently.

'Yes, I know it is! I heard you the first time.'

'Then you should try improving your telephone technique,' he said caustically. 'I'm back in England for a few days. Can you meet for lunch?'

'When?'

'Well, I was thinking of today,' he responded.

'Nice of you to give me so much notice.' Again!

'So you're busy today, are you?'

'Actually, no, as it happens—I'm not.'

'Are you trying to make a point?' he drawled.

Fran bit back the sarcastic comment which was looming temptingly on the tip of her tongue. No need to make him more grouchy than he already sounded. She made her voice saccharin-sweet instead. 'No point at all! Where shall we meet?'

'How about Green's? Do you know where that is?'

'Of course I do!'

'Good. I'll see you in there at one,' he said, and rang off.

Green's restaurant was situated in the middle of the Strand and famous for being famous, with branches in Paris, New York and Milan. It also prided itself on being impossible to get a reservation unless you were 'somebody' and Fran wondered if that was why Sam Lockhart had chosen it. To rub in just how important he was.

By the time she walked into the restaurant at just after one, it was nearly full and Sam was seated at a table towards the back of the room, which commanded a fine view of everything, but was well enough away from the general hubbub to provide privacy. Good table, she noted automatically.

He had been studying the menu but looked up almost as though he had sensed her approaching, his blue eyes briefly flicking over her, as though he was scanning a menu. And Fran felt a distinct disappointment. Because yes, if she was being truthful she *had* dressed to impress—and surely the way she looked deserved a bit more than that dismissive glance?

The mirrors lining the walls threw back her reflection. A caramel dress in softest cashmere, which clung to her curves and brought out the honey-gold in her hair. And high suede boots in glowing cinnamon, which had cost her more than a week's salary! Her hair was pinned into a casual chignon which had actually required a good deal of attention. She knew she looked polished and professional, but obviously not in the least bit sexy—not judging from that noncommittal response. But then, looking sexy was the last thing she was aiming for.

Wasn't it?

'Hello, Fran,' he said slowly, wondering if she *ever* looked unruffled.

'Hello, Sam.'

'Please sit down.'

'Thanks.' She slid down onto the chair opposite him, wondering if the deep blue of his suit had been chosen specifically to emphasise the dazzling colour of his eyes.

'Let's order straight away, shall we?' he suggested, with a swift smile. 'Then we can get down to business without interruption.'

'Okay with me.' She found herself nodding like an obedient dog, trying to look interested in the menu, when food was the last thing on her mind. She had never felt less like eating, and she wondered why. Guilt, perhaps? That she was here on false pretences? That she should find deceit so deliciously easy?

'What will you have?'

'Er, chef's salad followed by er, chicken, please.' She smiled rather weakly up at the waiter.

'Not hungry?'

'Not particularly.'

His mouth curved as he glanced at the lush lines of her body. 'And yet you look like a woman who enjoys her food,' he observed.

'Not when I'm working,' she lied. Normally she had no problem polishing off the most carbohydrate-filled concoction on the menu! But there was something unsettling about that bright gaze. She wasn't sure that her hands were completely steady, and the last thing she wanted was to send pasta flying all over her lap! Or to bite into a roast potato and have grease splatter all over her chin!

Once the waiter had taken their orders and poured water and gone away, Fran found herself growing restless under that keen stare.

'Everything okay?' he asked, wondering if she was *always* this jumpy.

'Oh, yes! Everything's fine!' She pointed to the briefcase by her feet. 'Um—I've had some of my press-cuttings faxed over from Dublin—which I thought you might like to see.'

His brow creased into a faint frown. 'Why?'

'Well, last week you mentioned that I had nothing to show you—'

'I doubt that I would have put it *quite* as inelegantly as that,' he objected, raising his eyebrows by a fraction, so that the crease in his brow deepened to a furrow.

Fran flushed. 'You know what I mean.'

'Yes, I know what you mean, but it's a little late in the day for references, surely? Especially since I've already given you the job.' His eyes glimmered. 'And am unlikely to change my mind about *that*. Unless you start committing unforgivable acts. Like wasting my time,' he finished deliberately. 'Again.'

Fran maintained a pleasant smile with the ease born of years of dealing with difficult clients and she could see that Sam was going to take first prize for being difficult. 'My time is as precious as yours, Mr. Lockhart—'

'I told you to call me *Sam*!' he grumbled.

'Okay. Then let's get on with discussing your needs, shall we, *Sam*?'

Sam was relieved that the waiter chose precisely that moment to deposit two plates of salad in front of them. Why, he wondered, did everything she say come out sounding like a sexy invitation? Especially when she definitely *wasn't* flirting. In fact, he'd go so far as to say that she was deliberately trying to avoid the instant physical attraction which had mushroomed between them at their first meeting.

Maybe that was why. He was so used to women coming on to him that it was novel, if somewhat confusing, when a member of the opposite sex kept sending out signals he simply couldn't recognise.... One minute she was hot, hot, *hot*. The next she was running scared.

He sat back in his chair and smiled. 'Okay. What exactly do you need to know?'

For one bizarre moment, she felt like asking him whether he had ever really been in love? Or whether women were just sport to him. Like some men hunted foxes, did he hunt women before moving in for the kill and then moving on?

Fran fished a notebook and pencil from her shoulder bag. 'Right. How many guests?'

'About a hundred and fifty. Strictly by invitation only.'

'Well, that goes without saying.'

'And definitely no gatecrashers,' he growled.

This bald statement gave Fran the first glimmering of an idea. 'Oh? Are you expecting any?'

'Maybe. You know what it's like. Think you can cope with them?' He seemed to relax and actually grinned at this point, and suddenly Fran understood exactly why Rosie didn't seem able to get him out of her system. Even after two years. He wasn't just gorgeous, she thought despairingly—he was absolutely *irresistible*!

'Yes, of course I can. Trust me.' Oh, heck! Her tongue had very nearly tripped over those lying words. Guiltily, she sipped at the water in front of her. 'Any ideas about the venue?'

'At my house in Cambridge,' he said immediately. 'I was thinking of a marquee in the garden.' He fixed her with a quizzical look. 'Though I guess it might be too cold to party in a tent in February?'

Fran shook her head. 'Not at all. They can make marquees as warm and as comfortable as palaces these days.'

'Can they now?' he teased.

'Um, yes.' Fran rapidly sipped some more water, wishing that he wouldn't look at her like that. Her cheeks felt so *hot*. 'But London would be a much better place to hold it, especially if you have people flying in from other countries to attend.'

Sam's mouth flattened. 'No way. If people can afford the air fare to travel to a ball, then they can afford the connection from London to Cambridge! And a hotel for the night.'

Fran flapped her notebook in front of her face, wishing that she had worn something cooler than the woollen dress. Did all women get hot and bothered around him?

'You're looking a little flustered,' he told her softly.

'I'm hot!'

'Yes,' he murmured as he allowed his gaze to drift over her flushed cheeks. 'So I see.'

His smile was so devastating that Fran felt quite faint. She drew an unnecessary question mark in the margin of her notebook and kept her voice efficient. 'We haven't discussed the proceeds,' she said.

'So let's discuss them now.'

'Er, have you decided whether you're going to donate the profits to charity?'

'As opposed to donating them to my Swiss bank account, you mean?' he asked drily. 'Actually, yes—I have. Every penny will go to the cardiology ward of the local Children's hospital.'

'Very admirable,' she said carefully. 'And, of course, paediatrics is always a very popular choice of charity.'

He narrowed his eyes. 'Why do I get the distinct impression that you're shocked?'

No, not shocked. Surprised. Because surely the type of man who ruthlessly treated women as sex objects wouldn't really be bothered about the plight of sick children? 'Why would I be shocked?'

'You think I've chosen a worthy cause just so it reflects well on me?'

'Now you're sounding paranoid!' she said nervously.

'I'm pretty good at picking up signals. And I'm getting a heavy sense of disapproval being directed across the table towards me at the moment.' He gave a bland, questioning smile as he poured himself a glass of wine. 'I just haven't worked out why.'

'Rubbish!' said Fran, as fervently as her conscience would allow her.

'Is it?' His eyes glittered. 'Anyway,' he put the glass back down on the table, 'I want as many doctors and nurses there as possible.'

Fran glanced down at the green leaves of rocolla which glistened unappetizingly on the plate in front of her. When she looked up again it was to still see those perceptive eyes fixed frowningly on her.

'Something wrong?' he enquired.

Fran shrugged, uncomfortable with her own thoughts. 'Well, doctors and nurses in England don't earn very much—'

'Don't I know it,' he agreed grimly.

Fran felt even more perplexed. The arch-heartbreaker was not supposed to feel sympathy for poorly paid employees of the service industry! Unless he was one of those men who was able to successfully compartmentalise his life. Just because he had an uncontrollable libido didn't mean that he couldn't have a soft heart, did it! Fran drew another question mark. 'But that means we'll have to keep ticket prices artificially low if they're to be able to afford it, doesn't it?'

He shook his dark head. 'On the contrary. Hospital staff will get subsidised tickets. Only the rich will pay more!'

'Gosh,' breathed Fran as the waiter took her salad plate away and replaced it with a perfectly poached chicken breast. 'You're a real little Robin Hood, aren't you?'

He raised his eyebrows. 'Now you *do* sound shocked!'

'Not many people care about financial inequality as much as you seem to!'

Sam frowned, his mind buzzing with all the mixed messages he seemed to be getting from her. He found himself wondering if she was always this prickly. And the prickliness intrigued him....

'Well, a variety of incomes guarantees a more lively mix, doesn't it?' he reasoned. 'And if you get the rich together—they seem to do nothing but compare incomes and complain about the service!'

Fran laughed nervously. Okay, so it appeared that he had something resembling a social conscience, too. Any minute now he would sprout a halo! 'How about colours for the marquee? Any preferences?'

'Nope.'

'Any specific food requests?'

'Nope.' He shrugged the broad shoulders and gave her a lazy, glimmering smile. 'That's what I'm paying you for, honey.'

'And my b-budget?' she questioned, her heart slamming against her ribcage.

He mentioned a sum and sizzled her a questioning look. 'How does that sound?'

Astute man. Fran nodded. 'You've pitched it just right. Unlimited budgets inevitably mean waste—and a limited budget always shows.' She looked at him curiously. 'What made you decide to throw this ball in the first place?'

'You mean I don't seem the type?'

'No, you don't.' People who threw balls tended *not* to be bookish recluses. And even Rosie had said it was completely out of character.

He shrugged. 'I met one of the local heart surgeons

at a party, and he told me that they could do so much more if they had more funds.'

'And so you decided to raise some? Just like that?'

'Just like that,' he echoed softly.

'Oh,' she said quietly.

'Oh!' he teased, and picked up a chip with his fingers. 'So that's the ball out of the way. Now what shall we talk about?'

She sawed mechanically at a piece of chicken. 'Pass.'

Sam leaned back in his chair and studied her, wondering what her hair would look like loose and falling all over her shoulders. 'You know, you're nothing like I imagined you would be,' he said slowly.

The feeling was mutual. 'And what were you expecting?'

'I thought that a party-planner would be outrageously glamorous—'

'Thanks very much!'

'The kind of person who looked like she partied non-stop herself.'

'And I don't?'

He shook his head. 'No, you don't.' She looked remote. Untouchable. The last type of woman you could imagine captured in the throes of passion on a very large bed. And consequently, the very person you wanted on that bed.... 'You look like you go to bed all clean, in a starched nightdress, with your teeth all brushed and minty,' he said huskily.

His voice stilled her, while his expression dealt a velvet blow to her heart. Something glowing crept inside her, touching a part of her she had thought Sholto had killed off forever. Oh, Lord—why hadn't Rosie warned her that she would be in danger of falling for him herself? Actually, when she thought about it—Rosie *had*

warned her. She had just thought she would be immune
to it.

Sitting in this gorgeous restaurant it was all too easy
to be beguiled by that lazy charm. To forget that he had
used it ruthlessly and manipulatively. 'Is that supposed
to be a compliment?'

'If you like. Is it true?'

Fran gave a ghost of a laugh. 'I have absolutely no
intention of telling you what I wear to bed!'

Her unwillingness to open up intrigued him, too. Most
women told you their life story at the drop of a hat. 'Did
you really use to work for a radio station?'

'Who told you that?'

'Cormack.' He smiled, as though he found it terribly
amusing. 'He said you'd been an agony aunt for a
while.'

'I'm afraid he's right,' she answered, wondering just
when they had had this discussion about her. And why.

'Unusual kind of job.' He narrowed his eyes. 'How
did you get into that?'

'In a very roundabout way. I was living in London at
the time and working in a big department store.'

'Boring job?'

'Very. I used to play netball with the girls every
Thursday night, and afterwards we all used to go to the
pub for a drink. One night we met a load of guys who
were over on holiday from Ireland. One of them started
telling me all his problems—'

'Was that your ex-husband?' he asked suddenly.

Fran nodded. Clever of him. 'Yes. He was working
part-time at the radio station in Dublin.'

'So let me guess—you gave him all the right answers
and sorted his whole life out for him and he fell in love
with you?'

Fran shook her head. 'Not quite. That's what you *don't* do. You direct, not dictate. People are supposed to choose their own solution to a problem.'

'And did he choose the right one?'

Fran remembered back. 'Yes, I guess he did,' she said slowly. Sholto had been unable to decide whether to follow his father into the family banking business, or to follow his heart and become a full-time disc jockey instead. She had asked him which was more important to him—his parents' approval, or his own sense of worth. Afterwards he had told her that in that one moment he had known that he wanted to marry her. And that had frightened her—to think that love could strike so randomly, so indiscriminately and so unsuitably...

'It's a nice story,' he said unexpectedly.

His crinkly-eyed comment threw her, made her feel even more of a fraud than she already felt. 'It had a nice beginning,' she told him quietly. 'It was just the ending which came unstuck.'

'Yes,' he said thoughtfully.

'When did you speak to Cormack?'

'After you came to see me.' No point lying about it, or being coy. She had aroused his interest, and he couldn't for the life of him work out why.

'What else did he tell you about me?'

He placed his hand on his heart, oath-style. 'I cannot betray a confidence, ma'am!'

She ran her fingertip over the rim of her wineglass, realizing that she knew very little about *him*—other than what Rosie had told her—and most of that had been about Rosie herself. 'How about you?' she asked coolly. 'Do you have any significant other in your life?'

'Why, will it cramp your style?' he teased.

She treated the remark with the scorn it deserved, by ignoring it. 'Have you?'

'Not at the moment.'

'But there must have been someone?'

His look was faintly incredulous. 'Of course there has—I'm thirty-two years of age, Fran! Surely you didn't imagine that I'd never had a serious relationship before? Do I look like some kind of loser?'

No, he didn't. Fran pushed her barely touched chicken away from her, something niggling at her consciousness. He had a way of answering questions which didn't add up with her image of him as serial seducer. 'I'm sure you've had loads of women,' she said lightly.

Sam frowned. 'No, not loads. Loads makes me sound indiscriminate—and I'm just the opposite.' His eyes glinted mockingly in her direction. '*Very* discriminate.'

'I'm sure you are,' she said politely.

Aware of the frosty vibes icing their way towards him, Sam wondered why he was getting the feeling that she was holding something back. 'So what do I need to do between now and the ball?'

She was aware of the sudden edge to his voice, and wondered if she was coming over as judgmental. She beamed him a megawatt smile. 'Just sign the cheques, Sam,' she replied, making every effort to sound her normal enthusiastic self and not a person in serious doubt of her own judgement. 'And turn up in your best bib and tucker on Valentine's Day!'

CHAPTER FOUR

FRAN stepped back to inspect the marquee and sighed with a kind of guilty pleasure. It looked magnificent—there was no other word to describe it.

The place was a riot of crimson and satin—red-swathed tables decked with hearts and flowers. Crimson roses adorned every available surface and romantic garlands of dark-green ivy seductively snaked their way up the pillars.

Was it too much, she wondered, narrowing her eyes and trying to view the decor with impartiality. No. It was perfect. The sumptuous interior did her justice. And she was glad that she had followed her instincts and opted for the traditional. After all, not providing red hearts and references to love on Valentine's Day would be a little like inviting guests for Christmas lunch and offering no tree or turkey! People would feel cheated!

There were three hours to go until the first guests were due to arrive, and so far—Fran superstitiously touched the wood of a chair back—everything was going according to schedule.

A delicious menu was in the process of being prepared by four chefs in the service tent adjoining the marquee. Hordes of waitresses were sorting out place-names, polishing wine-glasses and putting the final finishing touches to the tables. Soon the band would arrive. Almost every invitation had been accepted with the kind of disbelieving gratitude which might have been expected of a royal summons. And there were a few surprises in store....

Fran swallowed down her irrational fears. She had persuaded Rosie that less was more. That there was no need to overdose on the revenge bit. And that Mr. Sam Lockhart needed nothing more than a gentle rebuke to make him rethink the way he treated his women. A wry reminder of just how many notches he had managed to accumulate on his belt. That was all....

She nervously smoothed her hands down the bodice of the scarlet ball gown she had hired for the evening, then wished she hadn't. Her hands were all clammy and sweaty and it was more than just the usual pre-party nerves. To be honest, she would be glad when the evening was over. It had been hanging over her for weeks now with all the allure of an execution.

Still, Rosie had been pacified with her plan.

The DJ would play the record which Sam seduced all his women by. And one by one, some of those women would appear from the shadows and ask him to dance. Simple, effective and not *too* inflammatory. She hoped.

More importantly, Rosie had promised Fran that after tonight, whatever the outcome, she would get on with her life. Start living in the present instead of a bitter past or a wistful future. And cut down on the drinking.

'Hello, Fran,' said a soft, deep voice behind her, and as she whirled round to see Sam standing there, she gave a start of pleasure. They hadn't met since last month, for what was supposed to be a brief get-together. But he had taken her for an old-fashioned afternoon tea in an equally old-fashioned London hotel, and it had somehow gone on much longer than she had planned.

It had been the perfect antidote to the January blues—with scones and cream and outrageously fattening cakes and Fran had savoured the afternoon and his company with a guilty pleasure.

And they spoke on the phone most weeks. He had an easy and familiar way of talking to her which made her feel that they were old friends from way-back, rather than new and temporary colleagues. Dangerous.

'Sam!' She looked up into his eyes and found that she couldn't disguise her delight in seeing him. Now why this overwhelming feeling of pleased recognition towards a man she was supposed to dislike, and had met on precisely three occasions?

And why was he wearing *jeans*, for heaven's sake? And not just any old jeans, either—these ones looked like denim-coloured skin—the way they clung to those magnificent thighs and buttocks. Fran Fisher! she thought despairingly. What on earth are you *thinking* of?

'Why aren't you dressed, Sam?' she demanded.

A smile played at the corners of his mouth. He was surprisingly pleased to see her. But then she hadn't done what he had expected she would do. Plagued him with phone call after phone call. Invented all kinds of spurious reasons why she needed to meet with him. After a lifetime of women pursuing him, it was rather a relief to find one who didn't. For the first time in longer than he cared to remember *he* had been the one making the phone calls!

He stared down at the faded denim and the crumpled blue linen shirt he wore. 'It's true I look a little rumpled,' he admitted, with another lazy smile. 'But I'm not indecent, am I, honey?'

Fran blanched at the sexy undertone to his voice. Good! she thought. Make some more outrageous remarks like that! Remind me why I'm here. Reinforce that manipulative sex-appeal of yours so I don't get affected by that occasional glimpse of little boy lost in those big blue eyes of yours. 'I meant,' she said stiffly, 'you aren't dressed for dinner. And time is getting on!' She gave a repressive glare at her watch.

'Rubbish! We've got hours to go yet.'

'Three, to be precise. And there's still lots to do.'

'Well, while we're on the subject of clothes,' his eyes skimmed over the scarlet gown, pupils darkening into jet— 'aren't you a little…um…overdressed for last-minute checking?'

Maybe she was, but she had good reason to be. Sam had offered her the use of his house to get changed, and she had deliberately chosen to change early. Because the last thing she had wanted was to risk running into him outside the bathroom.…

The red dress she had hired was in richest velvet with a tight, boned bodice. From the waist, the material flared out over a stiffened petticoat, falling in great swathes of intense, glowing colour which brushed the ground as she walked.

Only her shoulders were bare—with lots of gold-flecked flesh on show. And she had been persuaded by the hire-shop to wear a strapless bra which pushed her breasts together, giving her an impressive cleavage which spilled over the top of her gown like overfilled ice-cream cornets.

It wasn't a colour or a style she would normally have come within six feet of, but the woman in the hire-shop had told her that it was perfect. 'You don't like it?' she asked him uncertainly.

He gave a small, disappointed laugh, thinking that women had a very devious way of inviting compliments. 'That wasn't what I said at all and you're smart enough to know it. If you're really interested—you look exactly like the heroine of an old-fashioned bodice-ripper. Or at least, you would if you let your hair down.' He gave her a questioning look and resisted the urge to run his tongue over his lips. 'Are you going to?'

'Since I have no desire to look like the front cover of a lurid book—no, I'm not!'

'Pity,' he said softly. There was a pause. The pulse in his temple begin to accelerate as he thought of how she *could* answer his next question. 'And what exactly are you planning to do between now and the start of the ball, Fran?'

Something in his eyes was making the tips of her breasts push hard and uncomfortably against the tight bodice. 'Oh, you know—'

'No, I don't. Tell me.'

She felt the breath begin to catch in the back of her throat and threaten to choke her. 'L-last minute checking.'

His eyes flickered over the straining swell of the bodice. 'Won't you be a little...' he paused, and his voice deepened imperceptibly. 'Hot?'

She felt her body reacting to the sensuality in his voice, even as her mind rebelled against it. This was how she had got into trouble last time. With Sholto. She had fallen for a lazy smile and an abundance of sex appeal. Silver eyes and a silver tongue. And just look where that had led her.... She fixed him with the kind of prim smile which an elderly schoolteacher might give to an unruly young pupil.

'Oh, no!' She shook her sleek, coiffeured head and not a strand moved. 'The temperature in the marquee is maintained at a steady degree throughout the evening—thermostatically controlled, of course! Right now it is comfortable, but it will obviously be lowered when the place starts to fill up,' she added helpfully. 'So none of your guests will get overheated, if that's what you're worried about, Sam.'

'That wasn't what I meant.' He gave a faint, perplexed smile.

She knew that, but sometimes playing the innocent was safer. 'I'm sorry.' Her voice was bright and interested as she gave him a brisk, professional smile. 'What exactly *did* you mean?'

'It doesn't matter,' he growled.

'Well, if you're sure…?'

'Yeah. I'm sure.' Oh, that prissy way she had of talking could be incredibly erotic, thought Sam achingly. 'Everything looks pretty-near perfect to me,' he murmured, finding that he couldn't tear his eyes away from the creamy expanse of her shoulders. There was something almost unbearably erotic about the contrast between the white-gold flesh and the glowing scarlet of her dress. Why didn't she dress in colours like that more often, he wondered? Instead of those drab, dreary shades she always seemed to wear. 'Just perfect,' he finished slowly.

'Why, thank you, Sam!'

'So why don't we go into the house and have a quiet glass of champagne before everyone arrives?'

She couldn't deny that she was tempted. Who wouldn't be tempted, for goodness' sake, when he had the knack of making a simple request to have a drink sound like an invitation to commit some kind of glorious and unforgettable sin?

She shook her head. 'I'd better take it easy. I have to drive back to London later and I'm not really used to the hire-car.'

'You don't have to drive anywhere,' he said tightly.

'There are four spare bedrooms in my house, all at your disposal. I can't understand why you won't stay.'

'I told you—I never stay over if it's just a one-off, like a ball. It's different if it's a house-party.' Which wasn't strictly true, of course. She *might* have stayed— and in fact she was going to have to come back tomorrow anyway. And it wasn't that she didn't trust him— that was the crazy part. She did—deep down inside, where it mattered. In spite of what Rosie had said. But she didn't know how angry he would be with her after the ball, or with Rosie. Or with the others. Whether he would accept the fairly innocent piece of revenge with good grace and a shrug of the shoulders. Or whether he would rage round the place like a rampaging bull!

After a lot of thought, she had decided not to risk it. Much safer to drive back and finish the clearing up to-morrow—once Sam had had the chance to see the funny side of things! 'Honestly, Sam,' she smiled. 'It's very sweet of you, but I won't.'

'How about a coffee, then?'

Oh, but he was testing her resolve! 'I really don't have time—and even if I did,' she let an apologetic note creep into her voice, 'it's a rule of mine never to fraternise with clients. You know? It sort of blurs the boundaries of the working relationship, particularly in this kind of business. And that makes for complications. I'm sure you'll understand, Sam.'

Sam couldn't remember having been snubbed so effectively for years. If ever. He felt a potent mixture of fury and frustration, and a sneaking kind of admiration....

'Forgive me,' he said faintly. 'I had no idea that I was stepping into the realms of the unacceptable. Maybe you're right. Champagne might blur my senses. And I have the feeling I'll need all my faculties about me tonight.' He gave a wicked and unrepentant grin as he saw her cheeks grow hot, enjoying the old-fashioned display of embarrassment. 'I think I'll go and relax in a hot tub.'

And with that teasing glitter lurking in the depths of his eyes, he turned away, leaving Fran staring after him wishing that she could rewrite the entire conversation and sneak off into the house with him. So much for being a strong woman!

Outside, waiters were scurrying in and out of the attached service tent where all the food was being prepared. Fran went and checked that the portable loos were up to scratch and on her way back into the marquee, looked up at the sky.

It was a clear, starry night—thank heavens. February was always a dodgy, unpredictable month where the weather was concerned. Rain was always a disaster. Hairdos got ruined. High-heeled shoes became stuck in rivers of mud. And female guests spent the whole evening with their teeth chattering. But rain on Valentine's Day was even more of a calamity—romance did not go hand-in-hand with the drowned rat look!

It seemed only minutes after Sam had left to take a bath that the string quartet arrived. The four musicians had been booked to play throughout the meal and afterwards there was going to be a disco, when the floor would be cleared for dancing. Fran organised a tray of coffee and cake, and left them to tune up while she swished round the room in her flowing red dress, nervously straightening a glass here, a napkin there.

She swallowed down the lump of anxiety which seemed to have taken up permanent residence in the back of her throat as she looked at all the place-names. Unsurprisingly, Rosie had not been on Sam's guest list. And neither had the names of the other women he had so cruelly dumped. Yet the list had been so varied and so balanced. There were authors, actors, doctors, secretaries, cleaners and even a used-car salesman! Fran had been reluctantly impressed.

'Well, hello, again, Little-Miss-Industrious.'

Fran looked up and found herself opening her mouth with instinctive pleasure as she saw just what Sam Lockhart had managed to do to a dinner jacket.

'Managing to keep yourself busy?' he murmured.

'Uh-huh. There's always something to do—if you look hard enough,' she gulped, wondering if he realised that he looked like the subject of a professional make-over.

But all men looked good in a dinner jacket, she reasoned. There was something about the colour and cut which slimmed them down, while the bow-tie made them look just old-fashioned elegant. But Sam needed no slimming down, or making elegant. What the jacket did for *him* was to emphasise the breadth of his shoulders, the length of his long, long legs and the darkness of the hair he had managed to tame into something resembling neatness.

But not quite. There was still something of the maverick about Sam Lockhart, something which no amount of grooming and expensive clothing could hide....

'Y-you've changed,' she said stupidly.

'Mmmm.' His blue eyes feasted themselves upon her bare shoulders again. What a pity she was working....

'But you haven't, I'm pleased to see.'

'No.'

'You should wear red more often,' he murmured.

Fran shot a desperate glance at her watch. 'They'll be here soon. The guests. In fact, oh, *look*—' and she felt almost dizzy with relief as she saw a couple standing at the entrance to the marquee, looking around them slightly uncertainly. 'Here are your first arrivals!'

'So they are.' Sam shot her a slightly bemused glance. 'You know, you're like a cat on hot bricks tonight, Fran,' he murmured, before lifting his hand in welcome. 'Do you always get this nervous before an event?'

If she told him no, he might justifiably wonder why. 'Of course I do!' she retorted. 'Nerves means that the adrenalin is pumping—which means that you're giving your best.'

'You mean this is the best you can do?' he teased, but before she could think of a reply, he was calling 'Monica!' and 'Nick!' to the first couple.

Fran was pleased to escape. The clammy feeling in her hands had increased, so that her palms felt slick and oily with moisture as the place began to fill up.

She drank a glass of water thirstily. Her task was almost over. Her duties nearly complete. Thank God. It was her responsibility to see that the evening ran smoothly—to remain visible and yet discreet. She was dressed as a guest, and yet she had not been invited. Her job was to remain in the background in case Sam wanted her. Her official role as spectre at the feast....

The meal passed in a blur. Fran watched the waitresses move around the tables like well-schooled puppets, smoothly replacing course after course. Most of the women simply picked at their food, which presumably was how they maintained their slender figures.

Fran's biggest anxiety had been about Sam's choice of partner. What if he had invited a simply lovely girl who would not only see the host get his rightful comeuppance, but who might be desperately hurt and upset in the process? She didn't want to think about it.

But to her surprise, Sam was partner-less. The woman seated at his side this evening was his secretary, Maria—a fine-looking woman, it was true. But Fran doubted whether even Sam would be having an affair with a woman nearly twice his age!

He had actually invited Fran to join him on his table—a mixture of the great and the good and several dignitaries from the local children's hospital. But she had turned him down flat and Sam wasn't used to being turned down.

'Why not?' he demanded.

'Because I'm *working*!' Fran had explained. 'If anything goes wrong—and by the law of averages it will, believe me—I'll have to keep jumping up and down to sort it out. Not very discreet in front of all your worthy and famous friends!'

Sam curved a reluctant smile. What she said made perfect sense. It was just that women tended to break rules where he was concerned and he found himself wanting this woman to do the same.

'And does your professionalism rule out a dance with your client?' he demanded.

Fran shrugged, her heart thundering, the voice of her conscience telling her that she really ought to say no. She ignored it. 'My professionalism says I'll consider it,' she answered lightly, thinking of at least twenty reasons why not. 'If you ask me later.'

Their eyes locked. He wondered if she had invented the phrase hard-to-get. 'Oh, don't worry, I will.'

So Fran ate her dinner on the hoof—bobbing in and out of the service tent, grabbing an oyster here and a succulent lump of lobster there. She admired the perfect strawberry-heart desserts, with the clever little chocolate curls made to look like arrows. Perfect Valentine fare.

'How's it going?' she asked one of the chefs, as they were preparing to decant the strong coffee into jugs.

'Like a dream,' he said, smiling. 'But that might have something to do with the amount of champagne they've put away. Funny, isn't it, that people drink the stuff like it's going out of fashion on Valentine's Day.'

'Well, it *is* supposed to be the stuff of romance,' shrugged Fran.

'If it's drunk in those quantities, it isn't!' remarked the chef raucously. 'In fact, it tends to have a very un-romantic effect!'

But Fran had noticed that Sam himself had remained moderate all evening, for he had none of the bright, flushed bonhomie produced by too much booze. Nor the smug righteousness of the abstainer, either.

She went back inside the marquee to find the tables being cleared, the string quartet bowing out after their second encore, and the man running the discotheque putting on the first dance number. Several couples rose to their feet and began to jig around rather self-consciously on the wooden dance floor.

Fran glanced at her watch. Just over an hour to go...

A shadow as dark as her fears loomed over her. 'Such a *troubled* face,' observed a deep, familiar voice. 'Is something wrong, Fran?'

'No! And I wish you wouldn't keep creeping up on me like that!' she said crossly.

He stared down at her consideringly. 'I could say that I wish you wouldn't keep jumping six feet into the air every time I approach you.'

Tension made her tactless. 'I'm surprised you're not used to having that effect on women!'

'How the hell would you know what effect I have on women?'

'Well, you're a good-looking man,' she said hastily, backtracking like mad.

'Now why does that sound more like an insult than a compliment?' he wondered aloud.

'I wouldn't want you getting a swollen head,' she told him sweetly.

'A swollen *what*?' came the innocent retort.

To her fury, Fran blushed and no words would come. No appropriate words, in any case.

'Oh, dear,' he murmured. 'You're determined to get hold of the wrong end of the stick tonight, aren't you, honey?'

'Stop it!'

'I wasn't aware that I was doing anything—other than trying to have a conversation with you. Any innuendo is entirely accidental. But that seems to be the effect you have on *me*.'

'Is that supposed to be a compliment?'

He shook his head. 'It was simply the truth. But since we seem unable to have a conversation without one of us inadvertently insulting the other—maybe you'd better come and dance with me instead,' he suggested gently.

'I can't!'

'Oh? Another rule?' he mocked. 'From the book of party dos and don'ts you wrote yourself?'

Fran studied the scarlet suede shoe which matched her dress perfectly. 'Something like that.'

'Well, let's break it, then. I hate rules.' He very gently put the tips of his fingers to her chin and tilted it upwards, not letting go, so that she was trapped by the blazing light of his eyes. Couldn't look away, even if she had wanted to.

'Come on, honey,' he murmured. 'Dance with me?'

He made it sound like a question, but of course it

wasn't. It was a beautifully-couched velvet command.
He knew that and she knew that. And it would be impossible for her to turn him down without making a
scene.

'The raffle,' whispered Fran frantically.

He frowned. 'What about the raffle?'

'This is the last chance for people to buy their tickets!'
she babbled, lifting her hand triumphantly from the vo-
luminous folds of her skirt and producing a book of tokens she was clutching. She waved them in front of him
like a ticket tout, producing her most winning smile.
'I've sold hundreds already, and now that people have
a few drinks under their belts, they'll dig even deeper
into their pockets! First prize a luxury weekend in Paris!'
she recited. 'Second prize a—'

'Okay, okay. I get the general idea,' he drawled, wondering if for the first time in his life she genuinely *didn't*
want to know. But Sam was astute enough in the ways
of human nature to know that whatever Fran Fisher felt
for him it was definitely not indifference. It was...
something...

He shook his head. Something he couldn't quite
fathom. Not when she was this close. He let her go with
a gracious shrug.

'How about after the raffle?'

Fran nodded, feeling like a born-again virgin! 'Ask
me again.'

'I will.' Sam moved away, feeling curiously relieved.
A dance in his current state would probably be the worst
idea in the world right now. Resistance and refusal was
more stimulating than he would have ever imagined and
he would hate her to see the physical effect it was having
on him.

Fran had never worked so hard to sell tickets, going

from table to table with her brightest smile, her most appealing eyes. Several men, too busy ogling her cleavage to pay attention, bought lavish amounts of tokens.

Slowly sipping from a glass of mineral water, Sam silently watched her progress from the opposite side of the room. She seemed distracted as well as committed, and genuinely oblivious to some of the more lecherous attentions she was being subjected to. He put the glass down and began to tap an impatient little beat on the linen-covered table, itching to haul some of those crass perverts out of their seats and throw them out of the marquee.

Some of them were old enough to be her father! Men he knew and usually respected. Made foolish and indiscreet by the ill-judged consumption of alcohol and the sight of a beautiful, unaccompanied woman.

But she was like a flower, he thought, flitting around in that bright, extravagant dress, her skin milky-pale in contrast. White and red. Innocence and experience. The drumming of his fingertips became insistent, matched only by a relentless pulse beating at his throat.

She was beckoning to him now, and he stood up stiffly to draw the raffle, moving towards her like a sailor to his siren. And suddenly, the world telescoped as she invaded his senses. All he was aware of was her standing close beside him, darting him those oddly shy little looks, her cheeks and her neck all flushed, like a woman in the aftermath of orgasm....

He was barely aware of presenting the prizes, of the sloppy kiss aimed at his mouth by one grateful female winner. By instinct he quickly turned so that kiss misfired and fell unwanted on his cheek, and all he could think of was how he wanted to explore the rose-red petals of Fran's soft lips. First the ones on her face, and then…and then….

He shook his head, like a man waking from a coma. He felt drugged or drunk, and yet he had barely touched a drop of alcohol all evening.

Without giving her a chance to say no, he reached out his hand in full view of everyone, taking her fingers within his grasp. He dipped his head so that he was close enough to speak without anyone else hearing. 'Now?'

To Fran, the word he chose sounded unbearably intimate. She knew she should refuse him, but she couldn't. And not just because to do so would have been unforgivably rude. But because she wanted to feel his arms around her. Just this once.

'Okay,' she nodded.

Maybe this, she thought despairingly as he led her onto the dance floor, was how Rosie had been with him. Powerless in the face of this much charm. Who *could* resist him?

He put a hand on each side of her waist, marvelling at the swell of her hips as they curved downwards in a soft arc. He pulled her a little closer and felt her shiver in response, and triumph coursed around his veins like lifeblood.

In his youth, egged on by hormones and predatory women, Sam had quietly engaged in the silent lovemaking which was considered perfectly normal on the dance floor. The instinctive thrust of the hips to show how hard he was. The cradling of soft flesh against hard male contours. Breath hot against long perfumed necks, while breasts would be crushed tantalizingly against the muscled wall of his chest.

But this dance was exceedingly proper. Hell, it was

proper! He was using the kind of touch he might employ if he was dancing with an elderly and shockable maiden.

And it was the most erotic experience of his life so far!

He had to do something—and not the thing which was uppermost in his mind. Much more of this slow enchantment and he would be dragging her off somewhere like a caveman!

He needed to talk to her, to do something to take his mind off how much he wanted her. 'So do you enjoy your work, Fran?' he attempted conversationally, thinking how bland he sounded!

Fran blinked as the words broke in to the slow flush of pleasure she was feeling. She struggled to concentrate. To resist the desire to unbutton the buttons of his jacket and to rest her head tenderly against his silk-covered chest. 'I suppose I do. But it's just a job—like any other job.'

'And what does that mean?' he wondered. 'Is that a yes, or a no?'

'Well, every job has its good side—'

'And what's yours? Apart from the obvious advantage of dancing with men like me!'

Fran's mouth twitched in response. 'Well, everything pales into insignificance next to *that*! But I like the freedom, I guess. I don't have to get up at seven o'clock every morning and put on a suit.'

The thought of her wearing some constricting little suit, with stockings and high-heeled shiny shoes, made the roof of Sam's mouth dry out. 'Yes, that's true,' he said evenly. 'And I suppose there's the inevitable bonus of going to lots of parties!'

She shook her head, her hair brushing silkily against his neck. 'Not really. Once you've done that a few times, you get it out of your system,' said Fran fervently. 'And believe me—parties and balls can become pretty boring after a while.'

'Well, thanks very much,' he said drily.

'Oh, not *this* one!' she corrected hurriedly, and then wondered if that sounded too gushing. Or too honest. She thought about the real reason why the last word she would have used to describe this night was boring, and blushed with guilt.

He saw the rise in colour which stained her neck, and an extraordinary sense of protectiveness washed over him. Sweet. He wasn't used to women blushing in his arms. 'You don't have to worry about saying what you mean, Fran,' he said gently. 'I'm not in the least bit offended.'

Fran stiffened. Oh, Lord! Any minute now and he would be! Why was he being so sweet to her? Why couldn't he do or say something outrageously sexist which would make her recoil? 'Good!' she said evenly.

He felt her grow rigid within his embrace, and frowned. Most women would have been gently parting their legs for him by now, waiting for the symbolic and proprietorial thrust of his thigh between theirs. The question silently asked and silently answered. Sam gave a grim smile and began to rub his thumb absently at the small of her back, feeling the pad brush against the scarlet bow which sat above the curve of her bottom.

The tiny movement was dissolving all her defences in a way which was totally alien to her, and Fran suddenly understood exactly *why* Rosie was overreacting. Just think of the effect he was having on *her*—still defensive and smarting from the failure of her marriage—after a few brief meetings and one innocent little dance. What on earth would it be like if he'd taken her out and showered her with attention? Kissed her? Made love to her? Fran shivered.

She turned her face up to look at him for one last time before the joke was played, her lips parting before she could stop them.

He couldn't resist. Couldn't. Just bent his head and brushed his lips against the shimmering bow of hers. Her eyes were open and so were his, hers so big and so dark that they looked like jet rimmed with a thin band of glittering green-gold.

He gave a lazy smile as he felt her mouth tremble beneath his. 'Mmmm,' he murmured softly. 'Want to lose the crowd? Find somewhere more private?'

It was probably the most innocent request he had ever made and yet Fran jerked back as if he'd asked her to peel her dress off in public. She gazed up at him, startled and shivering. 'Sam?'

Sam frowned. 'What's the matter, honey? Are you cold?' His voice was full of concern and he found that he wanted to rip the jacket from his back to cover those bare, creamy shoulders.

'No.' Just terrified. Because at that very moment Fran saw a frilly white handkerchief appearing round the tented flap which marked the entrance to the marquee.

It was the signal she had been waiting for. And dreading.

She moved her hand from where it had been splayed over Sam's chest and rested it lightly on his shoulder instead, so that she could see her watch.

Fran swallowed. It was time.

Sam felt her move. He was restless himself. The meadow-sweet scent of her hair and the rich feel of the velvet against his skin was unbearably stimulating to the senses. 'Want to sit this next one out?' he questioned huskily. 'Or dance on?'

'I think I've had enough dancing,' she told him truthfully. Much more of this and she would be blurting out what she had done.

'Me, too. You're a very distracting partner.' He cupped her chin in his hand, mimicking the gesture of earlier. His eyes crinkled as he smiled. 'At the risk of sounding terribly corny—do you want to save the last dance for me?'

'There must be someone else you'd rather dance with,' she said lightly.

'Nope.'

Their eyes were on a collision course and Fran couldn't have looked away, not if the world was tumbling about her ears around her. Come to think of it—in a few short minutes it might be doing exactly that!

'Fran, Fran, Fran,' he murmured. 'I'm blinded by the green-gold dazzle of your eyes but you still haven't given me your answer.'

'If you still want to dance with me later, then I will,' she hedged, knowing that the request would never be made.

She broke away from him and headed off in the direction of the white handkerchief, stepping outside into the crisp February air, her eyes adjusting to the darkness.

'Pssst! Fran!'

Fran turned round in the direction of the voice and she caught a glimmer of gold, heard a stifled giggle. Five women, all in evening dress, stood huddled beneath the shadows of a nearby tree like a coven of witches.

Only *five*? Rosie had implied that she would be bringing at least double that number.

Swallowing down her regrets, Fran carefully picked

her way over the foot-flattened grass towards them. Rosie was in the middle, wearing white, with most of her thighs on show and an air of suppressed excitement fizzing off her like electricity. The other four women were oddly disappointing. And not at all what she had been expecting. Over-perfumed and overmade-up, they looked cheap and out of place, like Christmas decorations brought out in the middle of summer.

And the last kind of women that she could imagine Sam seducing.

'Everything set?' Rosie whispered agitatedly.

Fran nodded gloomily. 'The song you requested will be played in five minutes' time.'

'Good!' Rosie gestured to the shivering bevy of women grouped behind her. 'Want me to introduce you?'

Fran shook her head. 'No, thanks. No offence, but I don't think I'm going to strike up any lasting friendships with any of you.'

'Is he in there?' whispered one of the women.

'Ask her,' answered a redhead in a silver jump suit, who pointed a talon-like fingernail at Fran. 'You were just dancing with him, weren't you? We all saw you smooching!'

Fran felt the accusation gathering up like a storm cloud as she faced five mutinous faces. 'I was *not* smooching!'

'No?' asked another spikily. 'We actually *saw* him kiss you, so I'd like to know what else you'd call it! Did you like the way it felt to have his arms around you, Fran?'

'He asked me to dance,' Fran said, realizing just how passive she sounded. 'What else could I do?'

A skinny brunette with bony shoulders narrowed her

eyes. 'Just be glad we're here,' she said huskily. 'And that we're saving you from certain heartbreak.'

Fran shook her head. 'I don't think I need rescuing.'

'You're trying to tell us that you *wouldn't* have ended the evening in bed with Sam?'

Fran shuddered with distaste and looked down at her watch, dreading what was about to happen next and yet longing for it to all be over. 'Your time has come, ladies,' she said, forcing a smile. 'Over to you.'

Afterwards, Fran tried to convince herself that it wasn't as bad as people subsequently made out. That it just happened to be bad luck that the floor had completely cleared as the evocative song began its first, sultry notes.

Sam was sitting chatting to a man at his table when Rosie appeared from nowhere and walked up with a dramatic kind of swagger to ask him to dance.

Fran saw him give a brief, perplexed look, as though he didn't quite recognise her. As if she was the last person in the world he had expected to appear. Which she probably was. But he appeared to hesitate only momentarily, shrugging his shoulders with a gracious smile as he rose to his feet to dance with her.

Maybe that would have been enough.

Maybe.

But one by one the four other women appeared from the shadows, each dressed up to the nines, glittering smiles pinned like tinsel to their shiny lips.

They surrounded the dancing couple, like wild animals circling just before the kill, and when Rosie moved away from him, another was ready to move into her place in Sam's arms.

Fran started to feel nervous. People must have sensed

that something out-of-the-ordinary was happening, because an odd, watchful silence had fallen over the guests.

And then Fran knew that she was in trouble, because Rosie had started staggering over to the discotheque, and had plucked the microphone out of the startled DJ's hand.

'Good evening, everyone! You have been watching,' she said, with the false, toothy smile of the professional television presenter, 'your host—the luscious Mr. Sam Lockhart—get his comeuppance at last!' She gave him a glassy stare. 'Because you can't just take a woman's virginity and dump her the following morning, and expect to get away with it, can you, *honey*?'

The deathly silence briefly rose into a murmur of confused question.

Rosie held up her hand for silence. 'This is to show you, ladies and gentlemen—' she hiccuped loudly and then gave an apologetic smile. 'But especially all you *gentlemen* out there—that if you trample all over a woman's heart and emotions as Sam has done—then you can expect to get paid back in full! We could have done a lot worse, but we decided that public humiliation was the best form of revenge for this particular snake!'

This part was totally unscripted! Fran shrank behind one of the ivy-covered pillars, hardly daring to breathe, wondering just how on earth he would react.

But Sam was nothing if not unexpected. His broad-shouldered shrug was more rueful than wrathful. Every eye in the place was on him as he lightly shook his silver-dressed partner away from him as if she were no more than a troublesome fly, and strolled across the dance floor to take the microphone from Rosie, who was beginning to look out of her depth.

'Ladies and gentlemen,' he said smiling, and Fran

could have heard a pin drop. 'I shall not attempt to defend myself, other than to say that it appears I have loved not wisely but too well!' There was laughter around the room at this, particularly from the men. 'However, the unexpected...' he shot a brief, hard glance around the marquee as if searching for someone, and Fran froze from her sanctuary behind the pillar. Had he *seen* her?

'The unexpected arrival,' he continued, 'of these very glamorous ladies shall not be in vain. Be sure of that,' he finished, on a note of soft threat. 'Very sure.'

There was a buzz of excited chatter, but his face grew serious as he looked around the attentive marquee. 'Tonight we are here not simply to have a good time, but to help with the enormous costs of running the cardio-thoracic unit of our local paediatric hospital. Several of the surgeons and nurses from that unit are here with us tonight, and I know that you will join me in wishing them well.'

He smiled again as the involuntary applause subsided. 'Each of these ladies will dance with whoever asks them. But at a cost. A generous cost.' His eyes glittered as they scrutinised the audience. 'And I'm here to take your offers. So who will open the bidding for the gorgeous creature in the gold-spangled dress?'

There was a roar of approval and excitement as three scarlet-faced men leapt to their feet, waving wads of money.

But Fran didn't care what happened next. The ball had been a stupendous success—anyone could see that—and from the clamour around the marquee it was going from strength to strength. She would forgo being paid. Forgo anything. All she knew was that there was no way she was going to be able to face Sam Lockhart. Not tonight. Maybe not ever.

Stealthily grabbing her bag and the satin-lined scarlet wrap which she had hired to match her ball gown, she crept out of the marquee and round to the side of the service tent, standing as still as a statue while she waited to see whether he had followed her.

But he hadn't.

She picked up her skirts and began to run through the darkened garden towards the designated car-park, her breath puffing like clouds of smoke on the chill night air.

At Sam's insistence, she had left a holdall with warm clothes inside the house. He had told her she should get changed before driving back to London, but she wasn't risking going into the house to get them. What if Sam came looking, and what if he *found* her? What then?

Hands shaking with fear, she located her car, slithered into the front seat and started the engine. And only when she was moving did she expel a long, frozen breath of fear as she bumped her way across the cold, quiet lawn.

CHAPTER FIVE

FRAN focussed then refocussed her eyes, glancing down at the fax which had just come spilling angrily off her machine.

Another one!

And this one hadn't even bothered to *attempt* to sound polite! Her eyes flicked over it. Drone, drone, drone... and then the explanatory and telling phrase, 'we are sure you will understand our reluctance to continue with our agreement under the circumstances. Discretion is the by-word for a small, family business such as ours and any bad publicity—'

Fran gave a howl of rage before crumpling it into a tiny ball and hurling it to the opposite side of the room where it bounced off the wall and joined two others on the carpet.

Why hadn't she *thought* of this? Why hadn't she even *considered* that organizing a stupid stunt like the one she had allowed Rosie and her cronies to play on Sam would be bound to misfire on her, and her alone?

Fran thought back to that awful night—was it only eight short days and not a lifetime since it had happened?—when she had sped back to London in a mud-spattered evening dress, ruining it in the process and incurring not just the wrath of the hire-shop, but a huge bill into the bargain.

She had taken the first available flight over to Ireland, and gone straight away to see her friends Fergal and Patsy, who lived halfway up the side of a mountain in

County Sligo. She had told them the whole story of the ball, and instead of looking outraged, they had simply laughed.

'Sure, and wasn't it just a bit of fun?' Patsy had giggled.

'Maybe,' said Fran hopefully, wondering why she didn't find their words more reassuring.

Of course Patsy and Fergal had not seen that frosty gaze as Sam's eyes had swept around the marquee like an ice-axe—searching for *her*, no doubt. Oh, *why* had she cowered behind the pillar, instead of meeting that accusing stare head-on? She could even have gone one step further and joined Rosie and the others, had the courage of *their* convictions and told him that he was a no-good rat.

Except that the image of Sam as a no-good rat was one which was stubbornly refusing to be real any more. From the first time she'd met him it had been an image which had never seemed to fit.

Fran had gone back to her own flat, expecting to find that he had sent her some kind of furious communication. By fax. Or phone. Or e-mail. Or solicitor's letter...

But there was nothing. Not from Sam. Zilch. Just the faxes telling her that as a party-planner, her days were numbered.

Fran sighed. She may not have heard anything from the man who had the most right to be angry, but she had heard plenty from other people. The newspapers which had come flooding through her letter-box in the days following the incident, for a start.

It had made a very readable little piece on a quiet weekday morning, when there was no real news around. Mirroring the theme of a film which had been popular at the end of the previous year, the column had inspired a whole clutch of 'revenge' articles.

Arguments then raged across the features pages of the tabloid press for days. Did Sam Deserve It? screamed one. While another carried a photograph of Rosie drinking a glass of champagne and lying on a chaise-longue in a too-low dress, proclaiming 'I Still Love the Bastard!'

Fran looked at the photograph closely. For all the dramatic headlines Rosie looked as if she was enjoying every minute of it, judging by the picture. It looked like her broken heart was intact once more. Fran sighed.

Outside the streets of Dublin buzzed with life, while inside Fran felt as empty as a biscuit tin, with a feeling of loneliness she couldn't quite shake off. Not surprising, really. No work to keep her occupied—and not a lot of any in the immediate future, either. Not until all this fuss had died down, that was for sure.

No relationship, either, of course. Mustn't forget that. Funny how it had never seemed to bother her before. In fact, she had sworn herself off men when her marriage had collapsed. The slow, nagging pain of a divorce seemed to pervade every aspect of your life and Fran had decided that it was better to steer clear of men, than risk them messing up your life for her.

So what was different now?

Because one man had stirred her emotions up? And because that man would never look at her with anything but disdain ever again?

The doorbell buzzed and Fran pulled a face, tempted to ignore it. Who could it be, other than the bearer of yet more bad tidings? Another letter terminating a contract, perhaps. Or a panicky pronouncement from her neurotic landlord, maybe. Asking her how she was intending to pay her rent when everyone in the city knew that she wasn't working and wasn't likely to in the foreseeable future.

The doorbell buzzed again.

'*All right!* I'm coming!' she called crossly, tightly knotting the belt of her gold kimono.

She didn't use the peephole, or the chain—but maybe that was because Dublin had always felt so utterly safe to her ever since she had first gone to live there. She pulled the door open and there stood Sam blocking out just about every bit of available light. But then, he was a big man.

Fran blinked uneasily. 'Sam,' she said cautiously.

'Yeah,' he said quietly. 'Sam. The man himself.'

Fran gulped. Yes, indeed.

As usual, he was dressed in denim—the jeans and jacket a bright, familiar blue. Underneath the jacket he wore a dark, roll-neck sweater which looked very soft. Unlike his eyes which were hard and bright. They looked like eyes which meant trouble, and Fran wished that she had enough guts to tell him to go away and then to shut the door in his face.

She saw that he was carrying the overnight bag she had left behind and when he noticed her looking at it, he dropped it unceremoniously at her feet.

'You left in such a *hurry*,' he emphasised sarcastically, 'that you forgot to take this.'

She pushed it against the wall with her bare foot. 'Er, thanks.'

'Well, Fran,' he said silkily, and she was appalled to discover how pleased she was to hear that honey-sweet voice. 'Aren't you going to invite me inside?'

Was he angry with her? It was impossible to work out from the look on his face just what he was feeling inside.

Still. He didn't *seem* too hostile.

His eyes flicked from the topknot of her hair, down over the clinging gold satin of the embroidered kimono to where her bare toes clutched the mat, like a swimmer about to dive. 'Or were you still in bed?' he drawled.

'No, I've been awake for hours.'

He pursed his lips into a mocking kiss-shape. 'But one doesn't necessarily rule out the other, does it?'

The Sam she had known would not have spoken to her with that curling distaste. If she had thought he wasn't angry, then she had misjudged the situation badly. Because he was. Not a shouting, screaming, banging-on-the-wall kind of angry, no. More a quietly bubbling rage which had a dangerous intensity all of its own.

Better to placate him than to antagonise him with a smart answer, surely? Fran tried a smile. It felt like a stranger to her face. But then, she hadn't exactly had a whole heap to smile about lately. 'You'd better come in! I…er…wasn't expecting you.'

'Weren't you?' he murmured, but there was an acid tinge to his words. 'Did you think I was just some poor punter you'd mucked around and made a fool of, and that I would quietly creep off into a corner, never to be heard of again? If so, then you underestimated me, Fran. Badly.'

She tried to imagine him creeping anywhere. It was a ludicrous idea! Fran shook her head, trying to appear calm, but it wasn't easy. She'd forgotten just what physical presence he had. And she felt especially vulnerable in this clinging kimono. She shook her head. 'I thought nothing of the sort! I meant that I wasn't expecting you to turn up on my doorstep at eight o'clock on a Tuesday morning. Especially not after all this time.'

'What—eight days?' he mocked. 'I decided to wait

until my anger had subsided a little.' He paused, and the look in his blue eyes was positively steely. 'I've always found that decisions made in the heat of temper are often the ones you most regret. I also wanted to be sure you would be in. That's why I didn't choose Monday—a notoriously unpredictable time to catch someone in—'

She stared at him uncomprehendingly. 'Why?'

'In case you'd been lucky, and scored at the week-end,' he elaborated. 'Although, maybe that's presumptuous of me—maybe I've disturbed a little early-morning lovemaking? Have you left some poor unfortunate high and dry in your bed panting for more?' His navy eyes peered over her shoulder in the direction of the half-open bedroom door. 'If so, I can always come back later?'

She knew then that she was trapped. There was no way on earth she was going to get out of this meeting. She had better just grit her teeth and bear it.

Wishing that she had gone with her initial reaction of shutting the door in his face, Fran stepped aside to let him pass, and her feelings of nervousness increased as she pushed the front door closed behind him. Should she excuse herself now and go and get dressed in something more substantial?

He hadn't waited to be invited in. Had just marched into her sitting room as if he were a regular visitor and was now standing in the middle of the room, completely dwarfing the place with his tall, denim-blue frame, his black hair looking tousled as it curled around his collar. He was squinting his eyes half-shut as he looked out of the window to where the Liffey was a faint, grey dazzle in the distance.

He turned around as she came in and she wondered could he see the faint shadows beneath her eyes? With so much leisure time on her hands just lately, she shouldn't have been tired. But tired she was.

'So,' she began cautiously, not daring to offer him a drink, because that really *would* be too hypocritical. 'You'd better get it over with, and say what you came for, Sam.'

As he turned, his fingers briefly skated over a large, round pebble she had found on the beach at nearby Dalkey and had brought home and polished.

'Please don't play dumb with me, Fran. It insults my intelligence.' He gave the glimmer of a smile. Only it didn't look the kind of smile you made when you found something funny. And his voice sounded different, too. Cold. Pithy.

'Sam, I—'

But he cut across her words as brutally as a scythe cutting through long grass. 'I realise now that my first instinct not to trust you was the correct one. You didn't just *hear* about the job, did you, Fran? It was a set-up.'

Fran opened her mouth to deny it and then closed it again. 'Yes.'

'Masterminded by a woman who isn't mature enough to know that rejection is part and parcel of most adult relationships! Particularly ones—' But he shook his head as he halted himself mid-flow, and walked back over to the window instead.

God, how cynical he sounded! 'I've known Rosie for years!' she defended. 'And I've never seen her in such a state over a man!'

'Is it my fault that women find me so irresistible?' he questioned, and Fran could have cheerfully punched him for his arrogance.

'No, but there are ways of dumping them which are

not guaranteed to break their hearts as you seem to have done!'

He turned around. 'Not if they don't want to hear what you're saying,' he contradicted softly.

Accusation burned in her eyes. 'Well, maybe Rosie took it so badly because it wasn't just her heart you stole!'

There was a long, loaded silence. 'What else did I steal, Fran?' he asked eventually. 'Her sense of proportion? Her powers of reasoning?'

'You know damned well what else!'

'Tell me!' he challenged, and met her accusing stare, head on. 'Go on! Say it out loud!'

She drew in a deep, shuddering, indignant breath. 'Rosie was a virgin before she met you!'

There was a long, odd silence. 'Oh, I see,' he said, nodding his head slowly. '*Now* I understand.'

'So you're not denying it?'

'That I was her first lover?' His mouth flattened as he shook his head. 'No, I'm not denying it. How could I, when it's true?'

Funny that it should hurt so much to hear him admit it. 'Well, at least that's one thing sorted out,' she said flatly.

'I'm just rather surprised that she told you about it, that's all.'

'Really?'

His eyes were piercing. 'Well, do *you* talk about your sex life with your friends?'

'No. Of course I don't.' Not that she had a sex life to talk about, of course.

'So you see me as some barbaric despoiler, do you, Fran? Plundering the treasures of innocent young women? Taking their virtue and then discarding them afterwards, like a piece of garbage? Positively medieval,' he mused.

Put like that, it *did* sound a little far-fetched. 'I didn't say that—'

'No. But that's what you meant.' His eyes bored into her. 'Or maybe you think I raped Rosie?'

'*No!*' She stared at him in horror.

Her vehemence was reassuring. 'Well, then—the logical conclusion to what you're suggesting is that because we had sex, then we should have got married. I don't think people travel down that particular road any more, Fran.' He saw the frozen expression on her face and his eyes widened in fascinated astonishment. 'I don't believe it,' he said softly. '*You* did just that! That's why you got married, isn't it? Because he took your virginity?'

'That's none of your damn business!'

'No, maybe it isn't.' But her face told him that his guess was accurate enough. 'What *is* my business, though, is how you and that pathetic pack of women attempted to sabotage a charity ball!'

Fran awkwardly rubbed her bare toes over the carpet. 'Look, Sam, it was just a case of five women playing a little joke—'

'A *little joke*?' he choked incredulously. 'Really? Making me out to be a serial seducer in front of friends and colleagues whose opinion I value? Forgive me if I don't share your sense of humour!'

'Rosie is a friend whose opinion I value!'

'But you didn't bother to check your facts, did you? What *did* she tell you, by the way?'

Fran's cheeks went the colour of brick. 'The same as she said at the ball—'

'Oh, you mean that charming announcement of being deflowered and dumped?'

'Which was unplanned, by the way—'

'Was it really?' he questioned witheringly. 'Sure you hadn't been rehearsing it together for days?'

'No! I had no idea that she was going to say that!'

'But you believed everything she told you, didn't you?'

'I've known her since we were at school together. Of course I believed her!' Her eyes flashed. 'Okay then, Sam—why don't you give me *your* version of what happened?'

He shook his head and gave a shudder of disgust. 'I wouldn't dream of talking about what I did with an ex-lover to a third party!'

Fran's heart plummeted. 'But you're not denying what she said? That you took her virginity?'

'No,' he breathed reluctantly. 'Those facts concerning Rosie are unfortunately true.'

Disappointment lanced at her skin like a million pinpricks. 'And she had four other women to back her up, all with virtually the same tale to tell!'

Now anger turned to disbelief. 'You think I took the virginity of all *five* of them?' he queried incredulously.

'I only know about Rosie!' she snapped. 'I didn't ask for a blow-by-blow account of just how far you went with the others—and will you stop smirking like that!'

'You have an unfortunate way of phrasing yourself,' he said drily.

'Well, whatever happened, you certainly made them angry enough to want to get their own back,' hissed Fran. 'Or are you saying that they *all* made up their stories?'

'I'm saying that they have pretty fertile imaginations! Or have you never heard the expression ''Hell hath no fury like a woman scorned!''?'

'What? A couple of scorned women I could believe! But five against one? At *least*! Oh, come on, Sam! The odds are pretty stacked against you!'

'Hell,' he murmured savagely. 'You really enjoy believing the very worst about men, don't you, Fran? Did your marriage do that to you? Did you decide to despise all men because one of them had let you down?'

Fran looked at him. 'Why don't you just tell me what happened?'

'I didn't lay a finger on any of the other four!' he told her softly. 'Did they *look* like the kind of women I'd be intimate with?'

She owed it to him to be one hundred per cent truthful here. 'Well, er, no. They didn't.'

'Even though they virtually offered themselves to me on a plate! Shall I tell you what really happened, Fran? Shall I?'

Fran nodded uncertainly.

'They all worked at Gordon-Browne when I was there—and they made no secret of the fact that they all found me sexually desirable.'

Which she could understand.

'Let me tell you—it was like having a permanently dark, dank cloud in the building with their dreary attempts at non-stop flirtation! They used to come on to me like second-rate hookers!'

'Then why didn't you have them sacked?'

'Because sacking four women would have been more hassle than it was worth! Imagine having to endure an unfair dismissal tribunal! Imagine all the publicity they would stir up by going to the *newspapers*,' he glowered pointedly. 'And by that time I had decided to go free-lance anyway so it wasn't going to be my problem any more. Besides, there was an exquisite kind of irony

'And how do you propose to do that? By having a personality transplant?'

For a person being offered what appeared to be a reprieve, she was bloody ungrateful! Sam felt an overpowering need to crush that indomitable spirit beneath his lips, and then to fill her so utterly that she would never again feel satisfied in the arms of another man. That would be both his revenge and gift to her....

'No, by spending a couple of days with me.'

Fran's heart clenched. 'Doing what?'

'What you do best. I want you to organise a small party for me.'

'You *are* kidding?'

'No, I'm not. I have no complaints about your organizational skills, Fran. Quite the opposite, in fact. The proceeds from the ball exceeded all expectations—the hospital went crazy with thanks. Several jaded socialites told me it was the very best party they had been to in ages—praise indeed. Particularly for the floor show.' His gaze was steady. Steady enough to notice that a pulse was flickering hectically at the base of her throat. And he wondered if that meant what it usually meant.... 'You're very good at what you do, Fran.'

She screwed her eyes up at him suspiciously. 'But won't people think it very strange for me to be working for you after all the adverse publicity? Won't they wonder why you're even giving me house-room?'

'No.' He shook his head. 'People will see us working....' he chose the next word with great care. He wanted to say 'intimately,' but that might frighten her off. '*Closely* together, and they will dismiss all the stories as rubbish.'

'And what if I say no?'

'Then I could make life very difficult for you.'

He said it almost pleasantly, Fran thought—and that made the simple statement all the more unsettling. She didn't doubt that he could make big trouble for her if he wanted to. And right now he looked powerful enough for anything…. 'What kind of party?'

His eyes betrayed no triumph—no emotion whatsoever. 'My mother will be travelling up from Cornwall, with my sisters. It's her birthday and I'd like to host a surprise dinner for her. Nothing big. Or fancy.'

'Your *mother*?'

'Well, I do have one. Don't you?' He gave a bitter laugh. 'It was the existence of my father which Rosie brought into question in that appalling newspaper article, and I'm afraid that once again, she got it wrong. He *is* dead—but he was very happily married to my mother for many years.' His mouth twisted. 'Sorry if that doesn't fit the stereotype either!'

'I wasn't the one who called you a bastard!' Fran protested.

'No, but you thought it, didn't you?'

She looked at him steadily. 'Are we going to spend the whole time raking up the fact that you think you've been misjudged by me, Sam?'

'No, I guess you're right. There's no point.' He controlled his temper with an almighty effort. 'My mother is going to be seventy. And I want to make sure she has a wonderful birthday. You can do that for me, can't you, Fran?'

'Well, I can,' she told him. 'But if she's seen the newspaper reports, then she may not be very happy about having me anywhere within a ten-mile radius!'

'My mother is an unusual woman. And never predictable,' he said, a trace of wry humour lightening his eyes. 'According to the sister who sent her Rosie's ar-

about telling them I was leaving and to see their hard, desperate little faces as they realised they would never see me again!'

Fran bit her lip as she realised that his version made far more sense. She believed him, that was the trouble. Every single word. Once she had seen the four women for herself, she had never really been able to imagine him being intimate with *any* of them. They simply weren't in the same league as Sam.

He narrowed his eyes at her. 'So why did you do it, Fran? I thought we got along fine together. Why think so badly of me? Why try and make a fool of me?'

Did he have a better nature to appeal to? 'Look,' she sighed and held up her hands in defence. 'It was a joke which—I agree—got out of hand. But it ended up doing you a favour, didn't it? *I'm* the one who looks like they're going to lose out. The bidding—which you began—raised an enormous amount of money for the hospital. No one thinks any the worse of *you*—'

'Other than my reputation as a stud being enhanced, you mean?'

'Okay, you may get a few offers!' she quipped recklessly. 'So what? You're now in the position of being able to pick and choose from any opportunities which may come your way as a result!'

Sam could never remember feeling quite so angry in his entire life. 'So you're completely unrepentant?'

She saw from the furious glitter in his eyes that she may have gone one step too far. 'Not completely, no,' she admitted. 'I certainly wouldn't do anything like that again!'

'Well, hallelujah!' he murmured.

There was a pause.

'So if that's everything?' she said warily.

Something in his voice put her senses on full alert. 'Oh?'

'Well, it's no secret that your business—if you can still call it that—is in danger of going down the pan. People don't like bad publicity. Clients have been pulling out of deals like rats leaving a sinking ship, haven't they?'

Pointless to tell a lie. He had obviously checked his facts. 'A few.'

'And your profession is the kind that stands or falls on its reputation, isn't it, honey?'

She felt an infuriating prickle of excitement when he called her that, even if the endearment was more snarled than whispered. But she shouldn't be surprised, not really. After all, Sam Lockhart's indisputable sex appeal was the reason she had gone charging to Rosie's rescue in the first place.

'Can't you see the writing on the wall?' he mocked.

'Get to the point, will you!'

'Okay.' Sam narrowed his eyes. 'Suppose I *did* sue you—it would be bye-bye to your business, wouldn't it?'

'Maybe it would! But it wouldn't be the end of the world. Not to me. Your threats don't frighten me, you see, Sam. No one has died. No one is ill. And I'm very adaptable.'

'I'm sure you are.' A pulse began to flicker in his cheek as he let his gaze drift slowly over her. He had wanted her to beg him, to plead with him, but her determination surprised him and intrigued him. Made the fight more equal. And the victory all the sweeter.

She had succeeded in making a fool of him, but more than that, had made him doubt his critical judgment. He had trusted her, warmed to her. For a man unaccustomed to giving either, it had been a shock to have them torn up and thrown back in his face. A unfamiliar anger had burned deep inside him, and he had forced himself to sit tight for days and consider his options. And not to take any action until he was in full control of his emotions.

Well, now he was.

'I'm sure you're many things,' he murmured, thinking how unworldly she looked, with her scrubbed face and clear eyes. It could be so misleading, a face devoid of make-up.... Only the sun-gold satin straining over the swell of her breasts and her hips reminded him of the siren's body beneath, and suddenly he wanted to possess that body. Possess it and ride it to glorious fulfillment.

She saw the blatantly sexual way he was looking at her, and felt her body begin to stir in response. Of course, if she had been expecting him she might have worn something a little more concealing. A satin robe with just a pair of pants underneath was provocative at the best of times. And no one in their right mind could describe this meeting as the best of *anything*.

She raised her eyebrows at him. 'So is that it? Have you said everything you came to say? You've tried to frighten me into fearing for my livelihood—and this, I guess is where you storm out again—to put the word around that I'm finished. The unforgiving victor, with just the sound of my desolate sobs shuddering in the background?'

Sam smiled. So she was a feisty adversary as well as being an extremely sexy one, was she?

'And what if I were to do the very opposite?' he questioned smoothly. 'To prove to you what a wonderful human being I am, and that Rosie and her rather pitiful acolytes were at best deluding themselves, and at worst...seriously deluding you.'

The Irish voice softened into a purr. 'Beautiful. Glowing like a jewel. And hardly showing at all. Just the tiniest swell around her belly, but she won't rest enough. I can see that I'm going to have to chain her to the sofa!'

'Or the bed?' suggested Sam.

Cormack laughed. 'Well, that too!'

'And Conor?'

The deep, Belfast accent became as soft as a pussy-cat's. 'The most incredible child ever to be born! As handsome as the day is long, and my heart's needle!'

Fairly safe to say, then, that Cormack's life was mill-pond smooth.

Sam opened his mouth and just lost it.

'That Fran Fisher—' he began menacingly.

Cormack interrupted with a whistle. 'Gorgeous, isn't she? In that very English way. Cool and collected. Never a hair out of place. The sort of woman where you wonder what goes on beneath the surface. You know, if I weren't a happily married man—'

'Cormack! You aren't listening! The woman is a conniving, manipulating, out-and-out—'

'Well, women are sometimes,' said Cormack indulgently. 'It's the way they're made!'

'Bitch!' Sam finished violently.

There was a stunned silence. And when he spoke again, Cormack's voice was positively frosty.

'Did you have something in particular you wanted to say to me, Sam?'

'Don't freeze me out, Cormack!'

'Then don't call a woman I like and respect names like that!'

Sam drew a deep breath. 'Well, *I* liked her, too!' he

stormed. 'I liked her a lot! Until she lied and cheated and tried to make a fool of me!'

'How?'

'*How?* Cormack don't you ever read the papers?'

'Never!' came the smug reply. 'What happened?'

Sam sighed. 'It would take more time and more energy than I have to explain. Remember that ball you couldn't come to because you were working?'

'Don't blame me for that, Sam—you missed Conor's baptism for exactly the same reasons!'

'I'm not blaming *you*! I'm blaming *her*! She set me up! She made me look a fool! And suffice to say that I'm mad. No, I'm not just mad—I want to get even!'

Cormack sucked in a long breath. 'Listen, man, the revenge thing never gets you anywhere. Ask my wife. If Fran has hurt you and got under your skin, then my advice to you is either to forget her—'

'Or?'

'Or marry her.'

'Or make her want me so bad that she can't forget *me*,' said Sam softly.

There was a long pause. 'Hell, Sam, what did she *do* to you?'

'She took from me something very precious, something that I didn't think existed any more,' said Sam grimly as he remembered the mushy way he'd felt when he danced with her. Feelings he had never imagined he would have for a woman again. 'And then destroyed it as surely as if she'd smashed it underneath the heel of her boot!'

'If you're thinking about revenge, I'm telling you again not to bother. There are more civilised ways to resolve things,' advised Cormack, in the tone of a man who knew what he was talking about. 'And trying to get your own back always misfires on you.'

'That's just what Fran Fisher is about to find out!' said Sam grimly.

'Sam?' Cormack chided. 'You're talking in riddles now! What are you planning to do?'

'She thinks I'm such a bastard!' Sam growled. 'Well, I'll give her something to really get her teeth into!' He shuddered involuntarily as he realised that the threat could feel exquisitely sensual.

'How?'

'I'm going to spend a night having sex with her!' Sam vowed. 'The most wonderful sex she'll ever have experienced in her life!' he added, knowing instinctively that it would be mutual.

'And then?'

There was a long pause before Sam spoke. 'And then...nothing. Just something to remember me by.'

Cormack sounded worried now. 'Listen, why don't you forget all that, and come out here for a holiday? Take your mind off things. We'd love to see you—Triss, especially. And Conor wouldn't object to being spoiled rotten, I'm sure!'

'Maybe I will,' said Sam, looking at the calendar with a gleam of anticipation in his dark-blue eyes. 'But not until after my mother's birthday.'

CHAPTER SEVEN

FRAN spent the next couple of days trying to contact Rosie and getting precisely nowhere. She wanted to know which story was true. Had Rosie's four colleagues made Sam's life a misery? Or vice versa? Except that she had a strong gut feeling which story would hold up.

But the message on Rosie's answerphone said she was out of town, and even her mother couldn't help.

'I'm sorry, Frances, dear,' she said down the phone. 'But she's gone off on holiday without telling me exactly where she's going. Most inconsiderate of her, especially when you think of everything that's happened in the last couple of weeks!'

'Yes,' said Fran glumly.

'But she seems to be much happier in herself, thank goodness. And she seems to be over that wretched man, Sam, at long last!'

Fran glowered at her reflection in the mirror. 'Er, yes. I expect she is. She didn't happen to mention who she was going on holiday with?'

'Well, that *is* the interesting part! Did you see the first article that was printed in the newspaper, the one all about her and Sam?'

'I certainly did!' said Fran vehemently.

'I didn't really approve of the language she used I must say, but she *did* look lovely lying on the sofa in that dress, didn't she, dear?'

Fran winced. How blinding mother-love could be sometimes! 'Mmmm!' she said encouragingly.

'Well, apparently the piece inspired a *huge* mailbag, and now the newspaper has flown her off to some secret destination, promising to find her a man as gorgeous as Sam Lockhart, only one who treats her properly this time. This I *would* like to see! I do hope she behaves herself, Fran,' she added worriedly. 'She's been drinking far more than is good for her just lately—and I actually thought that he looked terribly nice, this Sam Lockhart. Well, as much as I could make out from the snatched photograph I saw! He appears to have been scowling at the photographer. I can see exactly why she fell for him.'

'Er, yes.' Fran wondered whether that had been before or after he had threatened to land the photographer with a punch, as had been gleefully reported. Sam Lockhart was in terrible danger of becoming a minor celebrity, she thought with a sinking feeling of guilt.

'So when are you coming over to England next, dear?'

'I'm—' Oh, it would be much too complicated to tell Rosie's mother that she was calling from Eversford Station, having flown in from Dublin that morning. And even longer to explain why she was waiting for Sam to pick her up and take her to his house to start planning his mother's seventieth birthday party! 'I'm in a bit of a rush now! Can you tell Rosie that I'll call again, and that I need to *speak* to her! She can get me anytime on my mobile!'

She cut the connection just in time to see a mud-splattered four-wheel drive nosing its way into the station forecourt. No need to ask who was driving *that*! Fran felt the automatic clenching of her heart as she saw the rugged profile of the man behind the wheel. The dark hair which kissed the collar of the leather jacket.

He glanced across, saw her, and gave a grim kind of smile.

Fran walked over to his car just as he climbed out of the driver's seat, managing to turn a few heads as he did so, even though he was wearing nothing more sensational than faded denims and a beaten-up flying jacket. But he *did* look remarkable and the casual clothes did nothing to conceal his raw sex appeal.

His hair was windswept and his eyes sapphire-dark, and Fran remembered the feel of his arms around her waist as they had danced, his lazy suggestion that they should find somewhere private, and wondered what it would be like to go to bed with a man like Sam Lockhart.

She felt like an explorer entering uncharted territory. 'Hello, Sam,' she said quietly.

'Hi.' He kept his voice noncommittal, but he wished she wouldn't look at him with that solemn expression of expectation. He stared at her. In the cold, bright light of an early spring day he was discovering that it was going to be difficult to sustain the great rage he had felt while talking to Cormack. After all, she was here, wasn't she? Now it was all up to him....

'Good flight?'

Fran shook her head. 'A bit bumpy.'

'Pick up your connection okay?'

She nodded.

He wasn't sure that he liked her quiet and compliant like this. Looking like she was about to have her teeth pulled. He jerked his head in the direction of the station café. 'Do you want to get a coffee in there? Can't guarantee the quality, but it'll warm you up.'

She was more than a little surprised. After several sleepless nights dreading this confrontation, she had been expecting growled commands, not consideration. 'No, I'll be fine. We might as well get going.'

'Okay,' he nodded, silently observing her through the lush, dark curtain of his lashes, as he put her one small bag in the back.

Again, he was slightly perplexed at what she was wearing. Apart from that night at the ball—when she had been dressed to kill, and more—she was obviously a woman who believed that less was more.

She wore camel-coloured trousers which were casual, but definitely not jeans. He suspected that she would consider jeans unprofessional when she was working. And a big, creamy roll-neck sweater underneath a work-aday brown jacket. He wondered who had advised her to wear those neutral colours so that she merged into the background. Big mistake. She had looked utterly sensational in that scarlet ball gown. Maybe it was deliberate. Maybe she liked resembling the wallpaper. Blending in safely.

He looked at her white face and felt another irritating stab of concern. 'We'll drive with the window open. You look like you could do with some fresh air.'

'Why are you being so nice to me?' she demanded suspiciously.

'Because it makes sense.' He clipped the words out, allowing the mantle of hostility to settle around his shoulders with relief. 'You're here to work, aren't you? I need to keep you relatively happy, since I don't want you simmering away with resentment and glaring at everyone, just as we start singing "Happy Birthday" to my mother!'

She felt oddly disappointed, but didn't show it as she slithered into the vehicle. 'I would never be so unprofessional!'

He shot her a look as he climbed in beside her. 'But you think that arranging an ambush of embittered women falls into the category of professional behaviour?'

She didn't answer, but began edging away from him a little instead, thinking that if his legs weren't quite so long and so lean, then she might be able to tear her eyes away from them!

He knew exactly what was going on in her mind. She was as aware of him as he was of her! It was written on every delicious pore in her body which those boring and staid clothes couldn't quite disguise.

'Do you often have to go and stay in people's homes like this?' he questioned, unprepared for the slicing sensation of jealousy at the thought of her alone in a house with some of the men of *his* acquaintance.

'I do if it's a proper house party involving several meals, and it's out in the middle of nowhere like this.'

He frowned. 'Isn't it strangely…intimate, staying with people you hardly know?'

She wondered if he had used the word just to embarrass her. 'No more intimate than groups of work colleagues who go away on conferences and stay in the same hotel and eat breakfast together, surely? It's just a job,' she told him, though that was not strictly true in this particular instance. This time it *did* feel strange. Not like work at all. And it was in grave danger of becoming—to use *his* word—intimate.

He drove out of the station and shot her a sideways glance. 'So. Pleased to be back in England?'

Fran almost smiled. Almost. 'I'll leave that to your imagination.'

'You'd rather be somewhere else?'

Anywhere! 'A beach in Tobago would do,' she said drily. 'But—'

'Beggars can't be choosers, right?'

'Right.' She found the sight of those long legs utterly distracting. Best to sidetrack her thoughts. She glanced curiously out of the window at the flat, empty landscape whizzing by. 'Why choose to live in such an out-of-the-way place?'

Sam changed gear. 'Well, I like the country and I need the isolation. Space and peace and quiet. These days I only go to London when it's absolutely necessary. Most people seem to labour under the misconception that literary agents spend their whole lives swanning around the world in the lap of luxury and pulling off film deals, when they're not lurching from boozy party to boozy party, that is.' He shot her a swift glance. 'What do you think I spend most of my time doing?'

Having sex, she wondered wildly, going hot with just the thought of it. 'Er—reading?'

'*Exactly!*' he enthused, pleased by her perception. Women were notoriously hopeless at understanding his job. He threw her another glance and saw that she was blushing. 'Why have your cheeks gone all blotchy, Fran?' he asked, with cruel candour. 'Surely you don't find the idea of books sexually exciting?'

'Well, some, of course,' she parried. 'Don't you?'

'Oh, yes,' he said softly, thinking that this visit was getting more interesting by the second. '*Ve-ry* exciting. Maybe we should compare choices some time? We could even have a private reading of erotic literature while you're here, what do you say?'

She suspected that he could make a train timetable sound erotic, if he read it aloud! 'I doubt there will be the time for literary analysis,' she said crushingly. 'So why don't you stop wasting time and tell me about the sort of party you want for your mother instead.'

He threw her an innocent look. 'But I thought that

was your department? To advise me. You had very definite ideas about the Valentine Ball, as I recall.'

'Balls are different—you can generalise.' She swept on, unwilling to dwell on an evening which still had the power to make her feel uncomfortable. 'Birthday parties have to be tailored to the person they're for. So you'll have to tell me something about your mother.'

He slowed down as they reached some traffic lights. 'Well, she's quite a lady,' he said, smiling.

The trouble was that the longer she spent with him, the harder it was to stay indignant. And harder still to accept that this was the man who had—by his own admission—robbed her friend of her virginity on a one-night stand. Yet a man who described his mother in such a fond way was the kind of man you couldn't help warming to. If he had raved on and on about her, she might have thought that he was a 'Mummy's Boy' and if he'd expressed nothing but dislike she would have had him down as cold and unfeeling. He'd managed to gauge it just right.

'Go on,' prompted Fran.

He turned up the narrow lane which led to his house. 'She was an actress—in fact, she still is. She does the odd voice-over and the occasional television commercial.'

'Would I have heard of her?'

'I don't know. You might. Her stage name was Helen Hart and she used to work in children's television in the very early days—'

'Helen *Hart*!' Fran's face broke into a smile as she remembered tumbles of curls and a mobile mouth which could contort itself into all kinds of funny expressions. Helen Hart was Sam's mother! 'Gosh! Didn't she used to be Rolly the rag doll on ''Tea-Time for Tots''?'

Sam grinned. 'Aren't you a little too young to remember that?'

'Of course I am!' she said severely. 'But it's a television classic! They're always showing those old black-and-white clips, and most people know Rolly's special tune, even if they weren't born when she used to sing it!' Her voice began to bubble over with enthusiasm. 'And, of course, she *must* have a birthday cake with Rolly on the top—no question.'

He thought how infectious her smile could be. 'I don't see how. They probably wouldn't be able to produce it at the local bakers—not unless you drew them a picture,' he said gently. 'It was so long ago.'

'You're probably right.' Fran smoothed back her already smooth hair. 'So I'll just have to make it myself, won't I? When is she arriving?'

'Tomorrow afternoon.'

'It'll be tight—but I'll manage it.'

The car was crunching up the drive towards his front door now and Fran felt fear and excitement all mingled up with this odd sense of her body feeling like it belonged to someone else.

Her clothes, which were good-quality clothes she had worn and felt comfortable in many times before, suddenly seemed all *wrong*. He looked so casual, and she looked so uptight.

She felt like a rat in a trap with the constricting rollneck sweater enveloping her face like a ruff and the camel trousers all scratchy against her legs. Her face was still flushed and hot and her hair felt too-tight in its restricting pins. She found her fingers were itching to creep up and loosen them, and yank them out so that the glossy, golden-brown waves fell in a liberated cascade all the way down past her shoulders.

'Here we are!' Sam stopped the car and saw her rosy cheeks and her frowning profile and wondered why she was so uptight. Was it because she could feel the sexual tension closing in on them like a storm brewing, the same as he could?

Bizarrely, he found himself asking, 'Do you always wear your hair up?'

Fran turned round, vexed by a question which somehow managed to sound as personal as if he'd just asked her whether she always wore a bra! 'Why?' she questioned acidly. 'Does it bother you?'

Crazily, he wanted to tell her that, yes—it bothered him a great deal. That he would never know a full night's sleep until he had seen and felt the silk of that hair lying all over his bare chest. He swallowed down the desire and tried to make the subject sound scientific. 'It would just be interesting to see what it looks like down.'

She didn't need his opinion. So why did she suddenly find herself seeking it? Her fingertips tentatively touched one of the restraining hairpins. 'You don't like it?'

'Not much.'

'Well, go on, then. You can't just make a statement like that without clarifying it! Why not? Does it make my nose look big? My chin look wobbly?'

He shook his head. 'Nope. It just suggests character traits which I don't find particularly attractive in a woman.'

Don't ask him any more, Fran. Just don't *ask*, she told herself sternly! 'Such as?'

He seemed as reluctant to answer as she had been to ask. 'Oh, you know. Neatness, inflexibility, uptightness.' He withdrew the key from the ignition, and shrugged. 'I guess that's why it's so provocative when a woman unpins her hair. It symbolises the removal of all inhibitions—' Sam cleared his throat, unable to believe what was happening to him! Much more of this and he would be incapable of getting out of the car without her seeing just how aroused he was. And wouldn't that just support Rosie's poisonous prejudices? The stud with nothing but sex on his mind! 'Let's go inside, shall we,' he suggested throatily as he reached over for her bag. 'And I'll show you to your room.'

Fran fumbled for the car door handle to follow him inside the house, trying to ignore what he had said, and the way he had said it. She wasn't stupid. And to ignore that a strong, sexual attraction existed between them would be extremely stupid indeed. Perhaps it was a good thing that his mother was arriving tomorrow! Mothers made naturally good chaperones!

The bedroom he showed her to was low and cottagey. In fact, the door frame was so low that she had to stoop her head when she went in.

It was also downstairs.

Sam saw her quickly hidden look of surprise as he threw the door open. 'Thought you'd want to be near the kitchen,' he explained.

Which was true. Unfortunately, it also created an unflattering image of herself bustling around the stove, her sleeves rolled up and smudges of flour on her cheeks! 'Oh,' she said faintly. 'Well, yes. I suppose that does make sense.'

He frowned. He had thought she would want to be as far away as possible from him. He had certainly considered it sensible to have her on a completely different floor. He didn't want her to be on her guard, wary and defensive.

'I'm putting my mother in the biggest guest bedroom

and my sisters will each have one of the others. That just leaves mine—' It took all the will-power he possessed not to give her the smoky smile which was threatening to play on his lips. 'And it seemed pretty pointless for me to move out of my bed, just for a couple of nights, don't you think?'

He said no more but the unspoken statement hovered as clearly on the air as if he had shouted the words out loud. That she had a choice where she slept....

It was a pretty room. Plain and simply furnished, it was painted white with dark-wood furniture. Several framed samplers decorated the walls and a beautiful burst of embroidered sunflowers hung over the bed itself.

Fran began to unpack her few clothes and to slide her underwear neatly into one of the drawers of the dresser. Just what was the matter with her? She was here because she owed him. And he wanted to show her—apparently—that he did *not* have his brains situated in his groin. So why did everything they were saying to one another sound as though they couldn't wait to leap into bed and start tearing at each other's clothes? Was that what people called animal attraction? Was this what he and Rosie had felt for one another? How it had all started?

While Fran unpacked, Sam clattered around in the kitchen making tea, mightily relieved when the telephone rang and he could focus his mind on something other than wondering whether her underwear was as uptight and starchy as her outerwear....

'Hello?' he barked.

'Hello, Sam?' came an exaggerated stage whisper. 'Is that you?'

It was Maddy, his youngest sister. An actress like her mother, and scattier even than her mother—which was saying something. Never was a person more aptly named than Madelaine Lockhart, he thought with slightly grim indulgence. 'Of course it's me! I live here, don't I? Who else would you expect to answer the phone?'

Maddy dropped her voice so that it was almost unintelligible. 'Mmmm Nggg Mummm,' she muttered.

Sam frowned at the phone. 'Is Mum there with you? In the room?'

'No!'

'Then stop talking in that incomprehensible voice! What's up?'

'Nothing's up! Just tell me where we're meeting for this birthday dinner which you've been so bloody evasive about!'

'I had to organise the...er...catering,' he said, sounding even more evasive. 'And we're not meeting anywhere. We're eating here. The dinner's going to be held here.'

'At your *home*?' screeched Maddy in disbelief. 'You mean, *not* in a restaurant?'

'What's wrong with that? Dining at home gives you more privacy and flexibility than a restaurant.'

'Don't be so flippant, Sam! That's not what I'm talking about! You can't even boil an egg—you know you can't! How you've lived on your own for so long, I simply *don't* know!'

'I eat simple food. Anyway, I can't help it,' he said, realizing that it was true. 'Suddenly I *feel* flippant!'

'What *is* the matter with you lately?' demanded Maddy. 'From being the personification of I-Want-To-Be-Alone, you start throwing your house open on every available opportunity!'

'A small birthday dinner for my mother,' he corrected

modestly. 'Hardly takes me into the league of big-time entertaining!'

'What about this famous Valentine Ball? The one that made all the papers and which my friends all read about! This from a man who shuns personal publicity! And I notice that neither of your two beloved sisters were invited!'

'Do you and Merry invite me to every social function which *you* have?' he asked reasonably.

'No! Because we got fed up with you persistently refusing to come! So what *has* happened to turn you from hermit to socialite overnight?'

'It isn't as simple as that—'

'I'll bet it isn't!' said Maddy. 'It must be a woman!'

'You couldn't be more wrong.'

'I'll bet it is!'

'Maddy—' he said warningly. 'What did you ring up about?'

'I want to know do we dress Mum up before we leave? Or should she pack her diamanté in her suitcase? What do we tell her?'

'Tell her that I'm cooking dinner for her.'

'And are you? Really?'

'Yeah. I am,' he said, suddenly smiling as he put the phone down.

Standing in the doorway, Fran cleared her throat to let him know she was there. She had removed the heavy donkey-brown jacket and redone her hair so that not a strand stood out from the gleaming topknot. Sam thought she looked as though she was about to take dictation.

'*You're* cooking dinner?' she asked. 'Not me?'

Sam stirred the tea and turned round. She'd obviously heard his conversation. He frowned, thinking that she looked sort of *right* standing in the doorway, for all that her outfit made her look so prim. It had something to do with the pink cheeks, the bright eyes. Curves in all the right places. Oh, he was going to enjoy taking her to bed....

'It would certainly make the birthday a surprise if I could,' he admitted, trying to calm down his lust.

'Can you cook?'

'Not so's you'd notice. But I presume you can?'

'Big presumption to make, Sam! You should have checked first. Some party-planners can't make a phone call without delegating the task of dialling the number to someone else! It isn't part of the job description, you know!'

He ignored all that. 'But you can?'

'Actually, yes, I can.'

'Then you could tell me how to cook the meal—'

'*And* make the birthday cake, organise breakfast kedgeree, set the table and organise the flowers? Perhaps you could provide me with some brightly-coloured balls and I can juggle at the same time!'

'I can't see you'd find that a problem,' he murmured, watching her breasts move as she waved her arms around like that.

'Flattery won't work, Sam.' Fran glanced down at her watch. 'But I presume you've bought most of the ingredients?' She gave him a questioning look.

'Ah!' He shrugged his shoulders. 'Now who is making assumptions? Maybe we'd better skip the tea and go shopping.'

'I've got a better idea—let's drink the tea and *then* go shopping!'

Sam poured them each a cup and wondered if he was turning into some sort of masochist. He found he actually liked it when she spoke to him like that. It certainly made a change. He wasn't being arrogant—merely accepting what was true—that most women seemed to develop a severe case of hero worship whenever he was around. And someone who worshipped you could never be your equal....

Shaking off her objections, he found himself helping her into her ugly brown jacket, aware of the faint scent of flowers from her hair which drifted into his nostrils and which stubbornly refused to leave them for the rest of the day.

CHAPTER EIGHT

THE fluorescent lighting hurt her eyes and the tinny piped Muzak assaulted her ears. Fran felt like she had just landed on an alien planet.

'What *is* the matter with you?' Sam felt compelled to ask, though he guessed it was a pretty crazy question. She doesn't want to be here, he told himself. That's all.

But her answer surprised him.

'I'm just not used to going round the supermarket with anyone.' Particularly someone who had insisted on pushing the trolley for her and who saw fit to walk at least three feet behind her, so that every time she picked up a carton of cream, or a packet of butter, she had to wait for him to catch her up. 'Can't you walk a little faster?'

Well, he could. But from where he was standing—or walking—he could take advantage of the magnificent sight of her bottom, pertly swaying from side to side as she walked down each aisle consulting her list. Maybe those slim-cut trousers *could* be sexy, after all! They certainly gave a tantalizing glimpse of each buttock as she moved.

It was most peculiar. In his mind he had done nothing but demonise her ever since the Valentine ball. And that in itself had bothered him. She had been like a stubborn little itch beneath his skin that wouldn't go away—and he badly wanted her to go away.

He had also thought that once he had succeeded in luring her back—so to speak—he would soon get her out of his system. So how come he was tamely trotting around a supermarket behind her, thinking about her delicious bottom? A pulse begin to hammer at his temple. This wasn't how he had planned to do things. Not at all. What on earth had made him offer to *cook*, for a start?

'If *I* were cooking this meal, then the shopping wouldn't be a problem,' said Fran slightly peevishly, as she realised that the store was fresh out of basil. 'What on earth possessed *you* to offer, I just don't know!' She frowned. 'And why are you staring at me like that, Sam?'

'Because—' Hell, he had forgotten how incredibly provocative it could be to have a woman echo your thoughts like that. 'Because I was thinking *exactly* the same thing myself!' he said, with a certain sense of wonder.

Fran willed herself not to warm to that indulgent little dip to his voice. 'Well, that's hardly an earth-shattering conclusion,' she told him repressively. 'Since we're both relative strangers walking around a shop together buying ingredients for a meal, it would be pretty odd if we weren't thinking about who was going to cook it, wouldn't it?'

Sam felt oddly deflated. He was used to women seizing on the odd complimentary crumb he threw them— grabbing at them with the dedication of vultures picking over a carcass! Had he expected her to be immensely grateful that he was employing her again, so grateful that she would just fall to her.... He glared at a defenceless head of celery as the erotic image dissolved, and just hoped he hadn't sent his blood pressure rocketing up too much in the process.

'Why *are* you cooking it?' persisted Fran, mainly because he had looked almost hurt when she had snapped at him just then. And she had found herself stupidly wanting to ruffle that thick, dark hair and tell him everything was going to be all right. How dumb could you get?

'Because I can't think of anything which will give my mother a bigger surprise,' he admitted. 'And because she's reached that stage in her life where nothing really surprises her any more. She's eaten at some of the best restaurants in the world. So it has to be good.'

'Well, you can't really go wrong with simple, fresh ingredients,' said Fran. 'Here!' And she threw a pack of almonds in his direction.

He caught it, placed it carefully in the trolley, then carried on pushing. 'So didn't you ever go shopping with your husband?' he asked casually, and wondered if he was going *completely* mad. He, who usually ran to the opposite ends of the globe once relationships started entering the realms of the personal, now found himself avidly interested to learn about her marriage!

Fran frowned, tempted to tell him to mind his own business.

Sam noticed the frown and picked up a newspaper and pretended to scan the front page. 'Of course, if it still *hurts* to talk about it—'

'Not at all,' she said stiffly, wondering if he had deliberately goaded her into being on the defensive.

'He didn't like shopping? Or he didn't eat?'

'Of course he ate!' Fran sighed. 'Sholto was a DJ—'

'He played records?'

She giggled in spite of herself. She had once naively said the same thing! 'They don't actually *do* that any more, Sam. It's all computerised, digital. It is on the radio, anyway.'

There was a pause.

'Go on, then,' he said.

'Go on, what?'

'Tell me more. About Sholto.'

She stared at him incredulously. 'Tell you about my ex-husband? Why ever would I do that?'

Anger came back like a gritty balm to rub over his skin. He held onto it with an odd sense of relief. 'It might even things up between us,' he grated. 'You seem to know a hell of a lot about *me*—while I know practically nothing about *you*.'

She supposed that he did have a point. And what harm could it do? After all, they were going to have to talk about *something*. 'Well, Sholto became quite famous in Dublin. It's a small city and the entertainment industry is correspondingly small. He hated going to the shops because lots of fifteen-year-old girls would come rushing up to him waving their autograph books. And occasionally some even more intimate items of clothing.' She shrugged awkwardly.

'So...?' He looked at her unapologetically. 'What happened? Why did you split up? Did your hours clash? Or did you just find that you were incompatible?'

Fran nearly hurled the pineapple she was holding, at his head. And yet, *why* did she never talk about it? Because she felt ashamed? Wasn't it more shameful to keep it all bottled up inside her like some dark, guilty secret—especially when she felt she didn't have anything to be guilty about....

'You're a very nosy man!' she complained.

'No, just interested.' His voice was a velvet snare. 'Go on, Fran, you know you're dying to tell me.'

Fran shot him a frustrated look. What a persuasive individual he could be! Was this how he had got Rosie into bed? And how best to describe her ex-husband without sounding like a Grade I bitch?

'Sholto was a big fish in a little pond,' she told him. 'Who happened to be amazingly good-looking and could charm the birds off the trees. Which he did. Frequently. The human variety, I mean.' She glared at him, just daring him to ask her any more. 'There! Does that tell you everything you wanted to know about the reasons for my divorce, Sam?'

It certainly made the picture a little clearer. She had married a philanderer, and the betrayal must have been even worse because he strongly suspected she had been a virgin when they married. Was that why she had so blindly gone along with everything which Rosie had told her, he wondered?

'I guess it does,' he said thoughtfully.

Fran felt curiously exposed. 'And what about you?' she questioned, more ferociously than she had intended.

'Me?' he asked blandly. 'What do you want to know about me?'

'Having quizzed me all about mine, how about telling me something about *your* love life?'

He savoured the moment in the over-held look they shared. But now, he reasoned, was *not* the moment to tell her about Megan. 'I thought you knew everything there was to know on the subject,' he said smoothly, picking up a huge box of Belgian chocolates. 'Shall we buy some of these, too?'

She swallowed down her indignation. She certainly wasn't going to *beg* him to tell her! 'Yes, let's!' she agreed, looking at the size of the box he had chosen with undisguised greed. 'I'm a bit of a chocoholic, on the quiet!'

Which, presumably, was why she had that refreshingly shapely body, thought Sam as he followed her towards the cheese counter—though, of course, he wouldn't dream of telling her that. Women were noto-riously touchy about being told that they had healthy curves!

With all the shopping bought and loaded into the Range Rover, they headed back to the house and Fran had a distinct holiday feeling. Invigorated. Uplifted. Almost relaxed.

She shouldn't be feeling like this, she reminded her-self. She was supposed to be here on sufferance—not enjoying herself!

'Now what?' asked Sam, as they carried the last few carrier bags into the big, warm kitchen.

'Now you unpack the shopping,' she told him sweetly. 'So that I can see where everything goes.'

The rest of the day was spent as congenially as it was possible to spend time with a man who essentially hated your guts, Fran decided. And there was a strange irony in her being able to give him step-by-step instructions on how to make beef bourgignon, and him almost meekly following them while she made his mother's birthday cake!

Fuelled by cups of tea and the occasional biscuit, the only interruptions they had were several frantic phone calls from one of his more talented but neurotic authors, whose new book was about to go up for auction. They worked side by side in the kitchen until nearly eight o'clock that evening, by which time the room was filled with the most wonderful smells imaginable.

'That's it!' Fran wiped the back of her hand over her forehead, leaving a splodge of flour behind. 'We can't do any more until tomorrow.'

'Right.' He was itching to brush the flour away, but he held back. Her proximity all afternoon had been spell-binding, and his body was in such a high state of desire that he didn't feel safe going anywhere near her. Something to douse this unbearable sense of need was what was called for. 'I think I'll take a shower now and then maybe ring out for some Chinese food? That's if you eat takeaways,' he looked at her, a question in his eyes. 'Or maybe you'd prefer to cook something yourself.'

'Or maybe not!' said Fran with a grimace. 'Actually, I *love* Chinese.'

'Yeah.' He couldn't stop himself. He reached his hand forward. 'There.' A fingertip brushed against her cheek and came away caked in flour. 'You've covered yourself in cake-mix.'

The feather-light touch felt like something much more sensual than the simple removal of flour. Fran saw the darkening of his eyes, felt the prickle of her body in response to it—and the danger which hummed in the air around them. She licked her lips. 'Do you....uh...just have the one shower?'

'No,' he said huskily, silently cursing the architect who had recommended the second bathroom. Though what was he expecting—that she would take all her clothes off and offer to share with him? Oh, yes please, he thought longingly. 'My room has an en suite. Feel free to use the one on the ground floor.'

'Thanks.' Fran maintained her composed smile until she was standing safely beneath the punishing jets of the shower, praying that the force of the water beating against her skin would rid her of some of her demons. Demons which took the shape of Sam as phantom-lover—and this in spite of everything she knew about him!

Back in her room and wrapped in a huge, fluffy towel, Fran opened the wardrobe door and surveyed the few clothes she'd brought with her. They were the normal selection she would take to a job like this, but to her dissatisfied eye they seemed lamentably few.

In the end, she put on the same camel trousers that she'd arrived in, but teamed them with a silky-looking gold shirt rather than the cream sweater. The house was well heated and she always seemed plenty warm enough whenever Sam was around!

She was just brushing her wet hair when there was a rap on the door, and when she opened it Sam was there, a printed menu in his hand, a look of query on his face.

'I'll order now, shall I—' He broke off in midsentence, and frowned. She looked...

Fran frowned back. 'What is it?'

'Your hair.'

She touched a wet strand as if she were touching a talisman. 'What's wrong with it?'

'It's loose,' he murmured, aware that his voice sounded slightly dazed. As if she were the only woman in the history of the world to have worn her hair wet and loose down her back! Yet the effect it had on her face was simply stunning—softening it, making her eyes look like bright green-gold beacons.

She deftly twisted a rope of hair between her fingers. 'I'm about to put it up.'

'No, don't.'

Fran looked at him. *'Don't?'*

'You look more relaxed that way.'

'Precisely,' she smiled repressively, then glanced down at the menu he was holding. Perhaps food would take her mind off the fact that he had left the three top buttons of his shirt undone and that the moisture from the shower was making his skin gleam like a precious metal. 'I like just about everything on the menu,' she told him briskly. 'So you can order for me, can't you, Sam?'

If any other woman had asked that question, he would have adopted a look of jaded cynicism. It would have seemed overly cute. Too dependent. Too girly-girly. But then, any other woman would have asked him in a simpering way which usually meant that they wanted you. Fran didn't. So was that because she just didn't simper? Or because she just really didn't want him?

'I think I can just about manage that,' he said drily, thinking that a drive to the Chinese restaurant might also ease the ache in his groin.

Fran was in the sitting room when he arrived back, bearing all the different foil containers. He dipped his head as he entered the low room to find that she had lit the fire and warmed plates and brought trays in for them to eat in front of the roaring logs. She had also, he was immensely disappointed to discover, put her hair back up in a constricting topknot so that once more she looked remote and untouchable.

'Okay to eat in here?' she asked him. 'The dining room seemed a little cold, and a little formal and I thought it was best not to use it before your mother arrives.'

'In here is perfect. Did you read my mind?'

'No, I'm just feeling tired and lazy!'

'Me, too.' He had been dreading sitting facing her across a dining table with candlelight creating intimacy and making his blood sing with desire.

They ate prawns and chicken and rice and noodles, with cold wine to drink. Afterwards, Fran sat eating a fig and picking at a small bunch of white grapes, aware that he was watching her. And liking him watching her.

She knew what was happening. She was falling for

him big time. And he was about the most unsuitable
candidate she could have picked, bearing in mind the
circumstances which had brought her here. He had said
that he wanted to prove he was a good guy at heart, and
he seemed to be succeeding. With honours! Oh, hell, she
thought, why did life have to be so damned complicated?

Sam drank more than he would usually have done,
but then he reasoned that he would need some kind of
sleeping aid tonight. He noticed that Fran was nearly
matching him glass for glass, too.

'Shall I open another bottle?' he asked.

She was tempted. Then shook her head. 'Better not,'
she said. 'I don't want to greet your mother with an
almighty hangover.' Which was not the real reason at
all. She was starting to feel woozy and pretty sure that
if she had much more, then she might relax a little too
much and find herself swaying in the direction of his
arms!

She watched him lick a trickle of grape juice away
from where it had made his lips all sticky. Just watching
him eat was like a lesson in sensuality, with those long
fingers pulling the succulent fruits from their stem.
Popping them whole in his mouth. White teeth biting
into firm, juicy flesh. How was he managing to cast this
powerful spell over her?

She sat up straight and shifted her bottom back a bit.
What would she be doing if she *didn't* find him the most
attractive man she'd ever met? Talking! She cleared her
throat, like an amateur about to make an after-dinner
speech. 'So what made you decide to become a literary
agent?' she asked him.

Sam gave a wry smile, recognizing immediately the
reasoning behind the sudden change of tone. 'Because I
love writing, I guess.'

'So why—?'

'Didn't I become a writer?' He resisted the desire to peel her a grape, and popped another in his own mouth instead. 'Well, I did. I wrote six novels—'

'*Six?*' she squeaked. 'And were they published?'

'Ouch!' He pulled a face. 'I'm used to adulation, not realism,' he told her drily. 'And yes, they were published—all six of them.'

'So what happened, did no one want to buy them?'

'Ouch again! You know how to hit a man where it hurts, don't you, Fran? Yes, some people wanted to buy them, and some even did! But not as many as I would have liked. I think I recognised that my books were *okay* rather than unputdownable! And rather than spend the rest of my life doing something at which I would only ever be mediocre, I decided to put my objective eye to good use. So I fought for authors whose work I *did* believe in. With some success,' he finished, not at all modestly.

Fran thought of the piles of manuscripts she had seen lying around his study. It would take a pretty long time to wade through all of *those*! 'It must be hard work?'

'Well, it's not like working down the mines.'

'And lonely?' she asked suddenly.

'Yeah. Pretty much.' He began to stack the empty cartons on the tray. 'But that's the kind of life I like.'

'And what about children?' she asked suddenly.

He hid his surprise. 'What about them?'

'Don't you want to have any...of your own?'

His eyes narrowed. 'Why Fran,' he asked softly. 'Is that a proposition?'

Which had the undesired effect of making her scramble to her feet. And taking her provocative body away from where it was sending his pulses soaring, and off to bed instead.

Sam sighed.

Alone.

CHAPTER NINE

SAM'S mother arrived at three the following afternoon, accompanied by her two daughters, when the taxi carrying them roared to an abrupt halt outside the front door, sending gravel cascading everywhere.

Fran stood watching in the hall as Sam pulled open the front door, just in time to see the car execute a screeching three-point turn, and he wondered if the driver was a frustrated rally-driver, or merely had a death-wish!

A glamorous redhead wearing a floppy velvet hat was leaning out of the back window. 'Hello, Sam, darling! Aren't you going to give your baby sister a kiss?'

Sam glared at the taxi driver. 'Weren't you driving a little fast!'

'Sorry, guv,' shrugged the driver, with an expressive jerk of his head in the direction of the seat next to him.

'I told him to,' came an amused voice from the passenger seat. 'It was a condition of my giving him a tip, so wipe that furious look off your face, Sam Lockhart!'

Sam pretended to glower in through the window at his mother, and then his face broke out into the most uninhibited smile that Fran had ever seen. Standing unseen in the shadows of the hallway, she felt her heart beating erratically.

'Mother!' he reprimanded sternly. 'You're nothing but a speed freak!'

The redhead was clambering out, displaying show-stoppingly long legs. 'I actually offered to drive us myself instead of catching the train—stop looking so horrified, Sam! But they refused to insure me without me having to practically take out a second mortgage—'

'Thank God,' breathed Sam, in a heartfelt voice.

'And just because I'm an actress, *honestly*! Why is the world so prejudiced against actresses?'

'I used to have the same trouble myself,' said Mrs. Lockhart with an indulgent smile at her daughter. 'They see us as flighty and undependable! Now come and help me out of the car, Sam!'

Sam shot her a rueful expression as he gently helped her out of the car. 'Forgive me for not offering,' he remarked. 'But I have to tread on eggshells where you're concerned. Once you berated me for hours for treating you like an invalid!'

'Oh, I was years younger then!' dismissed Mrs. Lockhart airily.

'Just two as I recall,' he answered drily.

'That's absolute rubbish, Sam!'

From her hidden vantage point, Fran was able to get a good look at Sam's family.

His mother was still—even at the age of seventy—a remarkably striking presence. Almost as tall as Sam, her finely-boned face was surrounded by iron-grey hair which still fell in the mass of curls for which she had been known in her heyday. She had all the bearing and natural grace of an actress, and it was easy to recognize the television star she had once been.

Madelaine and Meredith, known affectionately—'but not *always* affectionately' as Sam had remarked earlier—as Maddy and Merry, were as different as chalk and cheese.

The redhead in the floppy hat was Maddy, the actress, pin-thin and tall like her mother, wearing exquisitely embroidered clothes of clashing colours and lots of velvet and lace.

Merry, on the other hand, was dark like Sam, with fierce navy eyes and a sensual mouth which smiled more easily than her brother's did. A scientist by profession, she was a quiet woman, who was frighteningly clever, according to Sam.

Mrs. Lockhart was flapping one heavily-bangled hand impatiently. 'Now just where *is* this girl?'

Sam frowned. 'Girl? What girl?'

'Maddy says you've been acting very strangely and it must be due to a woman!'

Sam shot an acid glance in the direction of his younger sister who gave a smug grin in response. 'Well, Maddy—as usual, I'm afraid!—is engaging her mouth before she uses her brain! The only woman here is Fran Fisher, and she was hired to organize this birthday dinner for you.'

Fran thought it might be diplomatic to slip back into the shadows at this point.

'But Maddy also said that *you* were cooking!' said Mrs. Lockhart, looking at her son in confusion. 'So what will this Fran Fisher actually be doing?'

Fran reappeared at the door. 'I'll be setting the table, pouring the drinks and doing the clearing up,' she smiled. 'I'm Fran, by the way.'

'So Sam's playing wifey and you're playing husband?' said Maddy, looking directly at Fran with a twitch of her wide lips. 'How very cosy!'

'Shut up, Maddy!' warned Sam. 'And Fran's actually being too modest. She's made a birthday cake and has been teaching me how to cook—'

'Even cosier!' gurgled Maddy gleefully.

'Shut up, Maddy!' said Meredith softly.

Sam narrowed his eyes. 'Fran, come and say hello to my mother and sisters.'

He watched with some amusement as the women all began to size one another up while they shook hands.

'Why don't I take your coats?' asked Fran. 'And you can all go in and sit by the fire while I prepare tea. Oh, and very many happy returns, Mrs. Lockhart!'

'Why, thank you, my dear!'

Soon they were all settled in the sitting room, and when Fran walked in carrying a loaded tray, she found them looking the picture of contentment. Mrs. Lockhart was sitting in the stiff-backed chair by the window, leaning forward so that Sam could place a cushion at the small of her back. Merry was reading the newspaper while pretending not to, and Maddy was stretched out like a cat in front of the fire, peeling an orange she had plucked from the fruit bowl and negligently throwing segment after segment into her wide mouth.

They all looked up as Fran put the tray down.

'Milk or lemon?' she recited. 'And there are scones, fruit cake—'

Sam was suddenly by her side. 'Sit down, Fran,' he instructed. 'I'll pour.'

'So you're playing Mummy as well as wifey, are you, Sam?'

'Shut up, Maddy!'

Mrs. Lockhart accepted a cup of tea from her son and frowned at Fran. 'Aren't you the girl who arranged for a lot of Sam's ex-girlfriends to come and embarrass him at some dance or other?'

Maddy snorted with laughter, Merry merely raised her eyebrows while Fran flushed a bright and unbecoming red. Only Sam looked unabashed.

'It wasn't Fran's idea—'

She didn't want him leaping to her defence like that, particularly not when she didn't deserve it. 'But I allowed it to happen,' she said stiltedly. 'It was a joke that Rosie wanted to play on Sam—'

'Is this the same Rosie who was always writing you those letters?' quizzed Mrs. Lockhart.

Fran stared at Sam. 'What letters?'

He gave a dismissive shrug. 'I never discuss past affairs in detail. I already told you that, Fran.'

'I brought him up to be a gentleman!' said Mrs. Lockhart proudly. 'Just like his dear father!'

Fran stood up, feeling more confused by the second. She didn't need Mrs. Lockhart to tell her what she already knew. And her instincts told her that Sam was trustworthy, dependable and true. She knew that something didn't add up, but what? Had Rosie told her the whole story? Or just been selective in the telling of it? 'I'll go and make some more tea,' she said, glad to be able to escape from the curious eyes.

'Then you can show us to our bedrooms and we can go and unpack,' said Maddy, giving her brother an innocent smile. 'Are you and Fran sharing, Sam?'

'Just the cooking,' he said lightly.

In a way, it was easier having a house full of guests than being on her own with him, Fran decided. There were no loaded silences, no tense feelings as the bedrooms seemed to scream out their close proximity.

Sam came into the walk-in larder just as she was putting the finishing touches to the birthday cake. She had chosen to ice it there because it was cooler and out of the way. She didn't want to get underneath Sam's feet while he was cooking, and, to be perfectly honest, she found him too distracting to have around the kitchen!

He leaned over her shoulder to look as she piped a last curl of hair with the icing nozzle.

'Heck!' he breathed admiringly. 'That's absolutely *brilliant*!'

'I can only see the mistakes,' she said gloomily.

'Like what?'

'Well, the hair should be a bit more russet than orange, don't you think? But that's the best mix of colour I can manage.'

'You're a bit of a perfectionist, aren't you?' he teased.

'I…' She looked up at him with reluctant pleasure. He was smiling, and so was she, and their eyes had locked in such a shining moment that if it had been anyone else, in any other circumstances, then she might have actively considered the unthinkable. That she found another man attractive enough to want to make love with him. Something she would have recoiled from, straight after her divorce. 'Yes, I am,' she agreed evenly. 'And speaking of which—did you put the potatoes in the oven to bake?'

As a defuser of desire it was more effective than a cold shower, thought Sam, as he clenched his jaw, and nodded. Oh, not the question itself, but the way in which she asked it. The world seemed to be turning in on itself as, for the first time in his life, Sam was discovering that his inbuilt sex appeal which over the years had caused him more trouble than not, was simply not working. And ironically, that made his hunger all the sharper.

'Yes,' he retorted. 'And before you ask—the casserole is bubbling, the vegetables are prepared. The appetizer is ready and I've just taken the dessert out of the refrigerator! Anything else you'd like to know?'

'That's very good, Sam,' she said demurely. 'How

about the cheese? That needs to sit at room temperature, too—'

'It is!' he snarled.

Fran gave him a thoughtful look. Had everything in his charmed life always gone exactly the way he wanted it, she wondered? 'Do you think your sister likes me?' she asked suddenly.

'Which one?'

'Maddy, of course—'

'Why?'

Fran shrugged. 'Well, she keeps making comments which are designed to embarrass me.'

'You've only blushed once!'

'So does she?'

'What?'

'Like me?'

Sam sighed. 'I expect so. Maddy's an actress. She observes human behaviour, and sometimes the best way of doing that is to provoke a reaction—that's all she's up to.'

'Well, I wish she wouldn't.'

He gave her a considering look. 'Want me to have a word with her?'

Fran shook her head. 'Good grief, no! I don't want to be typecast as some kind of wimp who needs a man to speak up for me!' She glanced down at her watch and grimaced. 'And just look at the time! Is the shower free yet, do you know?'

He didn't miss a beat. 'Merry's in there at the moment I think,' he said steadily. 'But you're very welcome to use mine.'

'How very kind of you.' Fran kept her face neutral. 'But I think I'll wait.'

He didn't press it. He might just be tempted to offer

to scrub her back for her. Not, he decided, with an almost masochistic kind of pleasure, that he thought for a moment she would do anything other than look at him with that cool, school-mistressy air of hers.

And decline.

'She shouldn't be long.'

'Thanks.'

Fran showered and dressed in record time, and was just piling her hair on top of her head, when there was a tap on the door. 'Come in,' she said rather inaudibly, since she had two hairpins in the side of her mouth.

It was Maddy, dressed entirely in green suede. And somehow Fran wasn't surprised to see her.

'Sit down,' she gestured indistinctly.

'Thanks,' said Maddy, and raking her long fingers through the whorls of her glossy red hair, she plonked herself down on the bed.

Fran speared the last two pins into her hair and turned round. 'Yes, Maddy?' she said pleasantly.

'Do you always wear your hair up?' asked Maddy.

Fran smiled.

'What's so funny?'

'Just that your brother asked me exactly the same question. Yes, I do.'

'Why?'

'Because it's neat, and tidy. And often I'm working with food, and clients don't like to see someone with their hair all falling into the crème caramel!'

'And because it's controlled?' hazarded Maddy. 'And that's the image you like to project of yourself?'

Fran felt slightly irritated at this instant character assessment from someone who barely knew her, but she didn't show it. And mainly because she suspected that, like her brother before her, Maddy had hit on a fundamental truth about her character. 'Perhaps it is,' she agreed, and looked at her expectantly. 'I'm due in the kitchen about ten minutes ago, so you'd better say what it is you want to say.'

'It's about Sam, actually.'

'I rather thought it might be.'

'Are you…'

Maddy paused delicately, but Fran was damned if she was going to help her out. If you wanted to be audacious with someone you had barely met, then you shouldn't expect favours!

'Am I what?' she asked.

'Are you having a relationship with my brother?'

'No, I'm not.'

'But you'd like to?'

Fran sighed. 'Some people might find your line of questioning intrusive, Maddy—for all that he's your brother. Is there a reason for it?'

Maddy fingered the patchwork coverlet on the bed. 'I just don't want to see him get hurt.'

Fran's first reaction was to laugh aloud. But she didn't. 'Sam's a big boy now,' she said, almost gently. 'Who can take care of himself.'

Maddy nodded. 'I'm not talking about that woman Rosie—'

'Before you say anything else I'd better tell you that she's my friend,' warned Fran.

Maddy shrugged. 'Maybe she is. Anyway, she's got nothing to do with it.'

Resisting the urge to mention the time again, Fran sat down on the chair next to the dressing table and sat facing Maddy. 'What are you trying to say?'

'Just that Sam was hurt once. Badly. And I think it's made him wary of women ever since—'

'We've all been hurt, Maddy,' Fran pointed out. 'I've been through a divorce myself.'

Maddy shook her head. 'At least you went through the marriage bit and all the passion that went with it. Okay—so if it burnt itself out, it burnt itself out. Sam never got that far.' She bit her lip. 'He was engaged…didn't you know?'

Fran felt as though a chasm was yawning open at her feet. And she felt like someone forced to look down into it. Someone who was terrified of heights… 'No,' she whispered. 'No, I didn't know that. What happened?'

'She *died*!' Maddy looked up then, defiant tears burning bright in her eyes. 'We all loved her, and then she died. Sam nursed her almost to the end. She was lovely. Absolutely lovely. Accomplished. Perfect for Sam. Even when she was ill she used to sew things, embroider things. She gave them all to Sam.' She pointed to the sunflower tapestry which hung over the bed. 'She made that.'

'It's beautiful.' Fran remembered the cushion she had picked up on her very first visit here. The bruised look of pain in his eyes. So *that* was why he lived this lonely, bookish life—because he had never got over the woman who had died. It was like being given a piece of something corrosive to eat just after a huge meal, but Fran kept her face carefully composed. 'I've seen other things that she's done,' she said quietly, feeling glad she had sat down. She suspected her knees might have buckled if she had stayed standing, and yet the information distressed her far more than it had any right to. 'Why are you telling me all this, Maddy?'

'Because he likes you—'

'I don't think so!'

'Yes, he does. I can see it in his eyes! He's different

with you. There's something about the way he looks at you.'

Fran gave a smile which was almost wistful. 'Believe me when I tell you that you're mistaking affection for good old-fashioned lust. I think he finds me sexually attractive, and I think that what adds to the attraction is the fact that I'm not all over him like a rash. Which is what he's used to.'

'He can't help the effect that *he* has on women! It isn't contrived, you know, it's inbuilt. And he doesn't deserve what that woman—your friend—has been saying about him!' said Maddy bitterly. 'It makes him out to be something he's not!'

'I don't know about that. All I do know are that the facts about Rosie and Sam are indisputable—Sam admitted that himself,' said Fran steadily. 'But what I let happen at the ball shouldn't have happened. I can see that now. It started out as a simple prank—so I thought—and then it just gathered momentum, like a train running down the side of a mountain. But people will forget, they always do. And Sam will forget, too.'

'Yes, he will. So I can't understand why you're still here,' said Maddy.

And neither, to be perfectly honest, could Fran. The story about showing her that he was a good guy at heart didn't quite ring true. I mean, why *bother*, she thought? Surely hers was the last opinion he valued.

'After the Valentine ball, I owed him,' she told Maddy. 'It's a simple repayment of a debt, that's all.'

But Fran found that she had to pay attention not to ogle Sam as she and Maddy went along to join the others in the sitting room. But while she saw him in a new light, learning about his fiancée made her feel even more confused. Maybe that was the reason he was considered

cold and indifferent—because, at heart—he *was* cold
and indifferent. And the reason for that could be that the
only woman he had ever loved had been cruelly and
prematurely taken away from him. Some people never
got over something like that.

But she put it out of her mind in order to concentrate
on the birthday dinner. They started with champagne,
when they not only toasted Helen, but Sam's late father
and Fran felt her eyes growing stupidly bright as she
sipped from the crystal flute Sam had filled for her.

'What's the matter, dear?' asked Mrs. Lockhart softly,
who had noticed.

Sam had also noticed. 'I think Fran's father died last
year,' he said, meeting her eyes. 'This reminds her, that's
all.'

Fran was touched that he had remembered, and grateful when he created a diversion by opening another bottle of champagne which had been made in the year of
his mother's birth.

He also insisted that she sit down and join them for
the meal.

'Oh, Sam, I *can't*!'

'Oh, Fran, you *can*!'

'It's supposed to be a family occasion—'

'It's also supposed to be a celebration! At least having
you there will stop the evening degenerating into a predictable cycle of sibling arguments! And besides, what
else are you supposed to do—sit out in the scullery, like
Cinderella?'

'But you haven't got a scullery!'

'Well, then, that decides it! You *must* sit with us.'

She giggled. Had the champagne made her feel this
light-hearted?

The meal went perfectly, except for the carrots being

very slightly underdone, but as Fran pointed out these days it was considered trendy to serve them almost raw!

The pièce de résistance was the birthday cake itself, and Helen Lockhart got quite teary-eyed when Sam carried it through, this time, on Fran's insistence.

'But it looks just *like* me!' cried Mrs. Lockhart, in delight, and then shrugged. 'Or rather, me as I *used* to look.'

'You still look pretty good to me!' said Sam gallantly and they all clinked their glasses together.

It was midnight when Helen Lockhart and her daughters went off to bed, leaving Sam to help Fran to clear away. When she straightened up from stacking the dishwasher, it was to find him standing on the other side of the kitchen, staring at her intently.

'You're very quiet,' he remarked.

'It's been a long day.' But she had been thinking about the fiancée who had died. The woman who had lovingly embroidered the cushion and the sunflowers. It was a harsh thing to have happened to him. What would he say if she asked him about it?

He nodded. 'A very long day,' he echoed, still watching her, almost obsessively. There was something different about her tonight. Some extra dimension to her. Something in her eyes he had not seen there before. A strand of hair had escaped from the tight topknot, and had floated down to dangle around the long, pure line of her neck, destroying the ordered symmetry of her hair. He longed to reach out and stroke it away. 'Go to bed, Fran,' he told her softly. 'I'll finish up in here.'

She looked up at him, unable to hold back any longer. 'Why didn't you tell me that you had a fiancée?'

He stilled. 'Who told you about my fiancée?' he asked eventually.

'That doesn't answer my question.'

'Maddy, I suppose?'

'Does it matter who told me?'

'Very loyal of you, Fran,' he observed wryly. 'I suppose it doesn't, no.'

'You never talk about it?'

'No, not really. I don't see the point most of the time.'

'Too painful?'

He nodded. 'Something like that.' But he saw in her eyes something more than the snooping kind of curiosity, which was what he normally encountered. He sighed. 'The pain has mostly gone now—the not telling bit is habit more than anything.'

'I wasn't planning on asking you any more questions—'

'I know you weren't. And that's probably why I'm talking to you about it.' He flicked her an astute look. 'Though maybe you don't want to hear?'

On a slightly-deranged emotional level, no, she most definitely *didn't* want to hear. But the wise and mature woman she wanted to be, knew that she *had* to hear. 'Yes, of course I do.' Fran dried her hands on a teatowel and waited while he finished putting knives in one of the drawers.

'We first met at university when I was in my final year and Megan in her first. So long ago now,' he murmured as he looked back on the galloping years with a kind of disbelief. 'We had a brief fling at my graduation party, and then I left for London and I didn't see her for a long time after that.'

Fran nodded as she recognized the bond of young, shared passion. Powerful stuff.

'Megan came to my office to see me because she'd written a book, and knew that I was working for Gordon-

Browne. She brought the manuscript across to me, and I promised that I'd have a look at it for her.'

'And was it any good?'

Sam's laugh was tinged with sadness. 'The book was rubbish,' he said brutally. 'And when I told her so, she had the most terrible tantrum I'd ever seen. And after that, she decided to fall in love with me.'

'You make it sound like a clinical decision—'

'Maybe it was.' He shrugged.

'And one that you had no part in,' observed Fran, in surprise.

'Sometimes it *is* a bit like that, don't you agree?'

'Maybe,' said Fran thoughtfully, remembering how at first Sholto had felt secure in the stability she had provided for him. The same stability which had made him feel caged once passion had burnt itself out.

'I think my refusal to compromise my standards, by taking Megan's work on simply because I knew her, really appealed to her. She saw me as strong and unbendable.'

'And aren't you?'

He gave the glimmer of a smile. 'Not always, no. But we always give our lovers the qualities we want them to have.'

'Maybe we do,' she said thoughtfully.

'Didn't you do that with Sholto?'

'I'm not sure. What attracted me to Sholto was that he *needed* me. He was so wild, so artistic, so gorgeous, and yet he was attracted to mousy old me.'

'I think you're putting yourself down unnecessarily,' he said drily.

'Maybe I am,' she agreed. 'He was also the kind of person who was ruled by his emotions rather than common sense.'

'The opposite to you, in fact?' he hazarded.

'In a way, yes, I suppose he was. And all the very things which first attracted me to him and him to me—were ultimately the things which drove us apart.'

'I thought it was his infidelity which did that?'

Fran nodded. 'But he was only able to be successful with women *because* he was so sensual and so in touch with his emotions.'

Sam shook his head. 'I don't rate unfaithfulness as being successful with women, quite the opposite, I'd say. And if he was so in touch with his feelings, then why the hell didn't he consider that he was hurting *yours*?'

Fran smiled at the passionate defence, and thought that he had very cleverly turned the conversation away from him. And Megan.

'So when did Megan get ill?'

Sam grimaced. 'We'd been together about six months, just got engaged, when she started feeling tired all the time. At first, we thought that she might be pregnant.' He paused as his mind took him back. The initial stunned excitement coupled with sheer panic that there might be a baby on the way. 'But she wasn't. I nagged her to see the doctor, and when eventually she did it was like one of those bad dreams you pray you're going to wake up from.' He paused again, but this time his face looked ravaged. 'She was twenty-four years old and they told her that she had less than a year to live.'

Unnoticed, Fran poured them both a brandy from a bottle which had been used to flambé the bananas, and handed him a glass.

He drained the drink in one swallow, without seeming to notice that he had done so. 'She had test after test. Drug after drug. But every time we tried a new treatment, it dragged her down more and more. In the end, she refused everything except painkillers, she said that acceptance was an easier thing to live with, than false hope.'

'She sounds like a remarkable woman,' said Fran quietly.

He looked at her for a long moment. 'Yes. She was. Thank you.'

'For what?' she asked, surprised.

For being generous to a woman who had me when I think you want me for yourself, he nearly said. But he didn't. That might scare her away. And besides, he wasn't sure just how much she wanted him.

'For making my mother's birthday so successful. For being such a good listener. Shall I go on?'

'Oh, please *do*!' she said, laughing. 'You're doing wonders for my ego!'

While she was doing precisely nothing for his abnormally high levels of frustration! 'I don't know why I've unburdened my soul like this,' he confessed.

Fran smiled. 'Oh, that's easy. Because you needed to,' she said simply. 'You live in a world of fantasy, reading your manuscripts in your beautiful, isolated house. But you've got to let reality in sometimes, Sam. However harsh it may be.'

Much more of this level of understanding, and he would be straddling her over the kitchen chair! 'Just go to bed, Fran, honey,' he growled. 'Before I retract my offer of finishing the clearing up!'

She knew from the look on his eyes that to argue would be futile. She also knew that if he tried to kiss her, she would not protest.

But there was no kiss, and no protest and she was not the kind of woman to make the first move—even if he was the kind of man who wanted her to. Her bed awaited her, chaste and undisturbed. She would spend eight hours in it alone, as she had done last night. And to-morrow she would go home.

She thought that the silence which stretched out between the two of them seemed like a bridge—the kind made of wooden slats which swayed precariously whenever the wind blew.

A bit like life, really.

'I'll say good-night then, Sam.'

He smiled. 'Good night, honey.'

CHAPTER TEN

UNSURPRISINGLY, Fran couldn't sleep, and after a while she gave up trying, climbing out of bed and wandering over to the window to see what the stars were doing. She drew back the curtains and looked out.

Outside, the moon looked like a giant satellite dish in the sky, milk-bright and gleaming. How dark the trees appeared against that ghostly light, she thought. How flat and silent the landscape. She leaned her hands on the window ledge, and wondered what Sam was doing.

Sam had been unable to sleep and was genuinely thirsty. At least that's what he kept telling himself. So naturally he needed to go downstairs to make himself a drink. He moved as silently as a shadow only because he didn't wish to wake his elderly mother. Or his two sisters. All of whom needed their sleep.

And the only reason he walked down the passageway which lay *away* from the kitchen was because he thought he heard a noise. He definitely heard a noise. A soft, swishing noise like the sound of a curtain being gently pulled. And how could he be called any kind of man unless he investigated noises coming from the direction of Fran's room?

But when he crept silently and barefooted along the polished boards to stand outside the partially open door, it was to find that his heart and his stomach seemed to have fused somewhere in the region of his mouth.

It was like one of those films they hardly ever made any more, when you just forgot everything—*every-*

thing—except the person standing right in front of you who had invaded every single one of your senses.

She was wearing a long, pale sort of nightgown, worn high to the neck, and long to the ground. The sleeves were long, too, and gathered at the wrists, and the tip of the gown brushed the floor. If the window had been open, the wind would have blown the garment away from her in a diaphanous cloud, so that she would have resembled the figurehead of a ship, looking out to sea.

But it was her hair which captured his imagination most. Loose. Free. Spilling down her back like warm honey. And he knew that it was loose for the rest of the night. His breath caught in a small, choking sound.

She heard him, and turned, too dreamy with the sight of him to act like she wasn't used to dark, ruffled men appearing at her door, wearing nothing but a pair of jeans. Her heart began to plummet out of control, but this sense of feeling that this was somehow *meant* to happen, made her voice sound oddly calm.

'Hello, Sam,' she said.

He shook his head, fruitlessly trying to break the spell of her enchantment. 'Surprised to see me?'

Her eyes were slitted. 'No.'

He smiled at her lack of pretence. 'Can't you sleep?'

'No.'

'Me neither.' His eyes gathered her in. 'I was right about the nightdress.'

She looked down at the ghostly gown. 'Yes, you were.'

They stood staring at each other across the room, like two people seeing each other for the first time.

Sam felt the blood which thundered inside his head. 'Fran—'

She opened her eyes a little wider. If only her limbs didn't feel so heavy, her body so lethargic. 'What is it?'

He meant to say, 'You look beautiful,' but it came out as, 'I want to kiss you.'

It was so heartstoppingly simple and direct that the words made her shiver. She meant to say, 'Sam, maybe this isn't such a good idea'—but it came out as, 'I'm not stopping you.'

He laughed then, but with pleasure, not triumph, pushing the door quietly shut behind him as he began to walk towards her, to cup her face between his hands. 'You haven't asked me why I'm here,' he whispered provocatively.

'I thought you wanted to kiss me.'

'Yes. I do.' He paused deliberately. 'Among many other things.'

In the half light she blushed. 'Are you trying to shock me now?'

'No. I'm giving you the opportunity to kick me out.'

'And if I don't?'

'Then I'm going to spend the rest of the night making love to you, honey.'

Her eyes were like saucers, dark with question. 'But what about the others?'

He stiffened and scowled. He had thought she had worked through all that stuff about Rosie and the vultures. 'What others?' he growled.

'Your mother.' She could feel his breath warm on her lips. 'And sisters.'

'I'm not planning to make a noise,' he whispered. 'Are you?'

'No. *Oh!*' But it wasn't easy. Not easy at all. Not when he had started kissing her like that and running his hands down the sides of her nightgown, so that the fabric clung to her body like skin. She wanted to gasp aloud with sheer pleasure, because where his hands led, his mouth followed, lips warm and soft and seeking as they suckled her breast through the filmy material.

'Is that good?' he smiled against the damp fabric.

'Don't ask questions to which you already know the answers!'

He tightened his arms around her waist and she shivered involuntarily, because oh, she had missed the feel of a man's arms around her like this.

He could hear the distracted quickening of her breathing and made himself stop kissing her, smoothing her hair down as he tenderly kissed the tip of her nose, and then each cheek. 'Much more of this and I'm going to push you up against the wall and do it right there, honey,' he groaned.

Fran was so turned on she could barely speak. 'So?'

He laughed with anticipation, but shook his head. 'No way! Not the first time. Bed,' he said firmly.

'Bed,' she echoed, her whispered word fierce with need. Yet for all her bravado, she felt terribly shy as she let him lead her to the tiny bed, and he gave an exaggerated sound of horror as he stared down at it.

'Just a touch on the small size,' he observed ruefully. 'Maybe we should creep upstairs and find somewhere more comfortable.'

'Like where?'

'Well, the other bedrooms are all taken.' There was a pause. 'That just leaves mine.'

Fran swallowed with nerves. She had never seen inside his bedroom, and just the thought of it made her wonder how many women had clambered willingly between the sheets with him. She wondered if Rosie...

'No,' she swallowed, shaking her head so that she could shake the thoughts away. 'We might wake them.'

He saw the dark, scared look on her face, felt her tense beneath the arm he was holding her with and knew immediately what she was thinking. He turned her towards him and put both his hands on her shoulders.

'Now listen to me, Fran,' he said gently. 'And believe me when I tell you that there are no ghosts to lay in this house of mine. None. And I won't be any more specific than that. Do you understand what I'm saying to you? This is my sanctuary and my haven—'

She stared up at him, not quite believing what she thought he was telling her, hesitating over her words of reply. 'You're saying I'm the first woman you've ever brought here?'

'No, not the first. The only woman,' he corrected.

It was both a compliment and a declaration, so what jinx made her say, 'Except for Megan, of course.'

He shook his head. 'No, Megan never came here. I bought the house just after she—' He hesitated, the word still sounded faintly obscene on his lips. 'Died.'

There was a pause. Facts, however painful, could not just be brushed aside because you didn't want to face them. 'How long ago was that?'

'Nearly five years.'

'Oh, Sam,' Fran reached her hand up and gently grazed her finger along the faint stubble of his chin. 'Sam!'

It hit him hard—that tender touch, and this overwhelming need to possess her made him feel as vulnerable as a kitten. 'But Fran—' He forced himself to say the words which could deny him everything he wanted from her, and more.... 'If the thought of other women is always going to be there like a barrier between us, then maybe it's best if I just go now. It's crazy to start something if it's only going to be ruined by the past.'

She thought of him leaving her now, like this, and knew it was a complete non-starter.

Because Sam seemed fastidious where sex was concerned. She believed that, deep in her heart, despite what Rosie had said. And the better she knew him, the more she grew to know his fundamental decency. It all boiled down to whether she was going to let the fact that he'd had a brief fling with her friend affect her whole life? She shook her head. 'No. You don't have to go anywhere, Sam.'

He looked deep into her eyes. 'No ghosts to come between us, then?'

She wound her arms around his neck shyly. 'None.'

He groaned with pleasure as he drew her down onto the bed, peeling the nightgown up over her body as though he were slowly removing the skin of some very exotic fruit. 'Shall we take this off?'

'I think we'd better,' she nodded, holding her arms up like a child being stripped out of wet clothes.

Sam, consumed by the urgent need to possess her, was also aware of an air of almost primitive hunger. It all seemed new, uncharted. As though he had never done this before.

He unzipped his jeans almost ruefully when he saw just how aroused he was. Saw her looking at him with a mixture of awe and excitement.

'You know, this first time may not last long,' he confessed, as he lowered his head to flick a pink tongue wetly over her nipple.

Fran gasped and closed her eyes as he began to nudge against her, not realizing that pleasure could be *this* acute. 'Oh, I don't know,' she purred. 'One way or another, it's going to last all night.'

When Fran woke up in the morning he had gone. She lay naked and aching beneath the duvet for a moment while fractured memories of the night came flickering back into her mind, one by one.

They'd made love most of the night. She had a whole marriage to compare it with, yet it had been the best night of her life. So how guilty did *that* make her feel?

She looked for her nightgown which was lying in a heap on the carpet, and then at the clock. She sat bolt upright.

Ten o'clock!

And she was supposed to be cooking breakfast for Sam's mother and his two sisters before they caught the train home! She jumped out of bed, consoling herself with the thought that at least she had made the kedgeree the day before.

She risked a glance in the mirror and then wished she hadn't. Her rosy cheeks and sparkling eyes rather gave the game away. Well, she would just have to brazen it out. And that meant throwing her clothes on and acting like nothing had happened.

There was a sink in her room, and she made the best use of it that she could. The old-fashioned strip wash made her shiver, but she welcomed it. The goose-bumps brought her crashing back down to earth, and that was the place she badly needed to be if she wasn't going to give the game away to his mother, or his sisters.

She slipped into a pair of cream trousers and a simple cream sweater and walked barefooted towards the kitchen, to see if she could help.

Sam was standing by the Aga, frying bacon. Merry

was buttering bread and reading the newspaper, while Maddy was busy chopping a melon and adding it to a rainbow pile of fruit already heaped in a glass dish.

They all looked up as she came into the room, and she could hardly look Sam in the eye, she felt so self-conscious and so *obvious*!

'Good morning, Fran,' he said, with an innocent, sunny smile. 'Sleep well, did you?'

She might have glared if that wouldn't have given the game away. 'I was—er—a little bit restless,' she replied truthfully, feeling the world's worst fraud as she did so.

'I expect that's why you overslept!' observed Maddy, looking up from a decapitated kiwi fruit with a knowing smile. 'And can I just say that your hair looks much better all loose around your shoulders like that. Sam said you always wore it scraped up on top of your head.'

'Did he?' asked Fran, thinking that fantastic sex must have addled her brain completely—she *always* put her hair up!

'He certainly did!'

Now when had he said that, Fran wondered? And how on earth had the subject of her hair arisen during a conversation with his sister?

'Coffee?' asked Sam, giving her a crooked smile and a look in his eyes which said that he wished they could be alone.

'Please.' But Fran felt as though she had no right to be there. Redundant. The three of them looked like a unit, all busy working in harmony together. While she had been employed to cook the breakfast and had overslept like an adolescent! 'Don't worry, Sam, I'll get it.' She poured herself a large mugful. 'Where's your mother?'

'She'll be down in a minute,' he said, smiling.

'She overslept.' Maddy stared at her unblinkingly. 'Just like you.'

'Oh,' Fran swallowed nervously, wondering if she could get away with offering to walk to the village shop to buy milk. Anything to get away from this awful feeling of having been caught up to no good. 'Can I do anything to help?'

'What did you have in mind?' Sam shot her an amused look and Fran quickly discovered that it was easy to feel like a guilty teenager, even though you were a woman of almost twenty-seven!

And Sam wasn't exactly helping matters, she thought furiously! 'How about the rest of the breakfast,' she queried coolly. 'After all, I'm supposed to be the one doing the cooking!'

Merry looked up from the newspaper. 'Stop embarrassing the poor girl, Sam,' she said mildly. 'And concentrate on the bacon, instead—it's burning! Surprised you didn't notice, but I guess your mind was on other things, huh?'

He gave a yelp as he whipped the frying-pan away from the heat and Fran began to gather jams and marmalades and sauces and took them into the dining room, glad to get out of the room.

Breakfast was eventually served. Fran found the prospect of food curiously unattractive and Helen Lockhart yawned throughout the meal.

'Are you okay?' Sam asked his mother.

'I'm fine, Sam, *do* stop fussing! I'm not used to rich food and fine wines and very late nights, that's all.' She peered closely at him. 'Though, quite frankly, you don't look as though you've slept very much yourself!'

'No, you don't,' murmured Maddy mischievously. 'Why's that, Sam?'

'Oh, *do* shut up, Maddy,' he said indulgently, but he was looking so pleased with himself that Fran shot him a warning look across the table, terrified that he might announce to his mother and sisters the exact reason for his lack of sleep!

'So what are your plans?' he asked his mother instead, and held Fran's glare with an I-can't-wait-to-be-on-my-own-with-you stare of his own.

'Well, I'm having dinner in London tonight with Maddy's new man,' said Mrs. Lockhart.

'A new man. Hmmm, you've kept that very quiet, Madelaine Lockhart!' observed Sam. 'Is it serious?'

Maddy sighed and pushed away her half-eaten bowl of fruit. 'Yes,' she said, in a mock-tragic voice. 'I'm afraid that it is.'

'Don't tell me,' commented Sam, with a cynicism born of familiarity with his sister's chequered love life. 'It's another actor? Who has beautiful cheekbones, but no money? And bags of talent, just can't get a job?'

'No, that's just the trouble! He's not,' sighed Maddy again. 'He's…' she bit her lip before announcing mournfully, '…an investment banker!'

'A *banker*!'

Fran thought that Sam couldn't have sounded more astonished if his baby sister had suddenly announced she was marrying an alien who had just landed from Mars!

Mrs. Lockhart was laughing now. 'I think it's an exquisite irony that my free-spirited and artistic daughter, who has spent most of her adult life talking about financial inequality on the planet, should fall in love with a man I am reliably informed could pay off most of the national debt!'

'So you're…er…leaving soon?' asked Sam.

'Why, yes, darling, we are,' said Maddy, determined

to get her own back. 'But just to be diplomatic, you could *try* wiping that great big grin off your face! Anyone would think you were *glad* to get rid of us!'

Fran rose hurriedly to her feet. 'Er…more tea, any-one?'

'I'd love some,' Mrs. Lockhart said, smiling.

Fran escaped into the kitchen and put the kettle on, and wasn't at all surprised when Sam came into the kitchen minutes later, with a very satisfied expression plastered to his face. He put his arms around her waist and then bent his head to kiss her softly on the lips.

'Hello, beautiful,' he smiled. 'I didn't get the chance to say that to you this morning, did I? In fact, I didn't get the chance to say *anything* to you this morning! Shall we start all over again?' And he kissed her again.

She allowed herself to sink into the kiss for precisely three seconds, then snatched her head away. 'No, don't,' she whispered. 'Someone might come in and see us.'

'Well, we're not exactly committing a major felony, are we?' he teased. 'We're just two consenting adults doing and enjoying what comes naturally.'

Which was not the most romantic way in the world he could have described it, Fran thought rather disap-pointedly. 'I just don't want them to guess that we—'

'I think we may be a little late for that, honey,' he interrupted ruefully.

'Why, have they actually *said* something?'

'Nope.'

'Well, neither did we, so—'

'We didn't need to say anything.' He tilted her chin with a finger and looked down at her thoughtfully. 'The chemistry between us was obvious enough, and you'd have to be lacking in any kind of intuition not to have noticed it crackling around the breakfast table like electricity—'

'Which leaves them to draw only one conclusion!' Fran groaned.

'Which is?'

'That we spent the night together!'

He mimicked her wide-eyed look of horror. 'Oh, my goodness!'

'Sam, I'm serious!'

'And so am I, honey. So am I.' The chin-tilting finger became a chin-stroking finger. 'What we've done is nothing to be ashamed of, is it?'

'But won't your mother think—'

'My mother has spent most of her life as an actress—there isn't a lot she hasn't seen or heard of, you know. I'm thirty-two and you're what—'

'Nearly twenty-seven,' she answered, miserable that he didn't know. And that he should ask her a question like that at a time like this.

'Well, then. Of *course* nobody in their right mind would be shocked or surprised to learn that we're two sexually active—'

'Sam!' snapped Fran, furious at the unromantic way he was describing what she had considered the most perfect night of her life. 'Please don't say any more!'

He frowned. Usually he was good with words—brilliant with words, even. He had to soothe neurotic authors daily and spent hours bargaining with steely contract managers at publishing houses on behalf of his clients.

So why was he coming out with crass lines that even the most insensitive person would reject under the circumstances? Last night they had made love and today they badly needed to talk. He gave her chin a last, lingering touch and decided that this could wait until everyone had gone. Until they had the house to themselves and weren't hampered by the prospect of an audience bursting in whenever they were trying to have a private conversation!

'I have to take them all to the station,' he told her softly. 'And then we'll have the place to ourselves. How about that?'

Fran nodded.

'Hey,' he said softly, but at that moment there was a clattering sound coming from the direction of the dining room and she quickly moved away from him.

'Oh, look—the kettle's boiling!' she said brightly.

Fran was glad to have the breakfast things to clear away—it gave her something to do while Mrs. Lockhart and her daughters were preparing to leave. And whatever Sam said the situation certainly *felt* delicate. His mother might be the most unshockable, liberated and tolerant septuagenarian on the planet but it didn't alter the fact that Fran didn't feel right about openly cavorting with her son.

Sam came into the kitchen just as she was finishing loading the dishwasher and resisted the urge to cup his palms around those delicious, high buttocks. He cleared his throat instead. 'We're going, Fran.'

'I'll come and say goodbye.'

Mrs. Lockhart kissed her on both cheeks. 'I hope we see you again, Fran,' she smiled.

Maddy, who was sporting yellow ribbons in among the russet curls, gave Fran a questioning look, full of mischief. 'I rather think we will, don't you?'

'Well, if ever you need an event planned, I'd be happy to organise it for you.' Fran returned the cheeky look with a smile. 'Like a wedding or engagement party, for instance?'

Maddy went pink. 'We'll see.'

'Bye,' said Merry, giving Fran a quick, unexpected and very welcome hug. 'Look after my big brother for me.'

'He doesn't need any looking after,' answered Fran truthfully.

'Nonsense!' Mrs. Lockhart shook her head vehemently. 'All men need looking after!'

'Does the man in question get any say in all this?' asked Sam, with a grin. 'Because I have to say that I'm firmly on the side of my mother on this one!' He picked up his car keys from the hall table. 'Bye, Fran,' he said softly, his eyes luminous with promise. 'See you soon.'

'Bye,' she whispered back.

Fran stood on the doorway waving them off, and wondered just what would happen when Sam came home. Well, she had a pretty good idea of what might happen in the short-term, and she felt the slow unfurling of excitement as her mind painted erotic pictures inside her head.

But where did they go from here as a couple? He had made it clear that he wasn't promiscuous, but it would be wrong to read too much into *that*. And just because he had taken her to bed didn't mean that he was about to start proposing they move in together. Did it?

She calculated that it would take fifteen minutes to reach the station, and Sam would wait until he had seen them safely boarded on the train. Which probably left her with enough time for the bath she hadn't had time for this morning....

She was just unpacking bubble bath from her bag when there was a sudden loud ringing on the doorbell, and Fran looked with surprise at her watch. Surely that couldn't be Sam back already? No, impossible. And anyway, Sam had a key.

She opened the door without using the peep-hole and was slightly startled to see an unfamiliar broad-shouldered figure standing on the step, his dark-featured face scowling and angry.

'Don't you women *ever* use a peep-hole for security reasons?' he stormed.

With the sound of the musical Irish voice came recognition. 'Cormack!' cried Fran delightedly. 'Cormack Casey—the world-famous Irish screenwriter—as I live and breathe! What on earth are you doing here at this time in the morning?'

Cormack looked strained, Fran thought, but then the last time she had seen him had been at his son's baptism, which she had arranged, when he hadn't appeared to have had a care in the world.

'Can I come in?' he asked.

'Of course you can come in! I'll even make you some coffee, if you're lucky! Or breakfast. Have you eaten?'

But Cormack shook his head. 'Not now. I need to talk to Sam. Is he here?'

'No, but he won't be long. He's taken his mother and sisters to the station. He should be back in, say, half an hour.'

The lines of tension round the Irishman's mouth seemed to ease. 'Helen and the girls have been staying here?'

'Just for the one night.'

He looked watchful again. 'And how long have you been here, Fran?'

Fran frowned. Something wasn't right. 'Just the two nights. Cormack, is something the matter?'

He was one of the most decisive men she had ever met and yet now his face seemed to be cast in an agony of uncertainty. 'I hope not,' he said obscurely.

And suddenly Fran was fed up with feeling as though a play was taking place, only none of the action seemed to involve her!

'Cormack,' she demanded. 'Do you mind telling me exactly why you're here? And please don't say that you're just passing, because this isn't the kind of place that *anyone* passes.' Let alone a man for whom fame was the natural consequence of his success as a Hollywood screenwriter.

'I'm about to write a novel,' he told her gruffly. 'Sam has been on at me to do it for years. I can't keep putting it off. I've decided to write it now and I want to discuss it with Sam first.'

There was something about the way he was stubbornly refusing to meet her eyes. Something about the uncomfortable set of his shoulders. For a fundamentally truthful man, it must have been very difficult for him to try and lie to protect his friend, thought Fran.

'That may be so. But that isn't why you're here, is it?' she questioned insistently.

Their eyes met.

'No,' he said at last.

'I think we'd better go and sit down, don't you?'

He followed her into the sitting room, shaking his head with the air of someone who had a heavy burden resting on his broad shoulders. 'Triss told me not to come,' he sighed heavily.

'Well, you clearly ignored your wife's advice,' said Triss sternly. 'And now you're here you'd better start explaining.'

He narrowed his eyes at her, as if trying to read her mind. 'How *is* Sam?'

If she hadn't spent most of the night with Sam exploring her body both inside and out then she might have been able to answer the question without blushing as deeply as she could ever remember.

'Oh, *hell*!' snarled Cormack, before she had even had a chance to answer. 'Hell!'

Fran stared at him in pink-cheeked confusion. 'Cormack? What on earth is the matter?'

'Time is,' he shrugged. 'I'm too late, I guess. You've already—'

She frowned as he bit his lip and seemed to change his mind about what he was going to say. 'Already what?'

'It doesn't matter.'

'Oh, I think it does—certainly to me. So what was it, Cormack? You know you're going to have to tell me.'

He ground the words out with difficulty. 'Have you...slept with him?'

She was too shocked to be offended by the question. 'I think you'd better explain yourself,' she said quietly.

He shook his head. 'Just forget I ever asked.'

But something in the almost *defeated* slump of his shoulders both alarmed and unsettled her. And made her determined to get to the bottom of what was making Cormack look so uncharacteristically troubled. 'I can't do that. Not now. You know I can't. You've opened up a can of worms, we can't just close it again.'

'Let's wait for Sam.'

'No, let's not.' She gazed at him steadily. 'I'm waiting, Cormack.'

'Yeah.' He shrugged, and tried to play it down. 'I was just a little bit worried about you, that's all—'

She narrowed her eyes suspiciously. 'You came all the way here from Ireland because you were worried about me—'

'No. I had business in London as well.'

'So would you mind letting me into the cause for your concern?'

'Listen, Fran,' he screwed his face up awkwardly. 'I like Sam—'

'No, Cormack!' she cut across him furiously. 'Stop telling me half of what I want to hear! I want the truth—plain and unvarnished—not all dressed up with praise for your friend!'

'Okay.' He ran his hand distractedly through the thick, black hair, making it even more untidy. 'He told me he was angry with you after the ball. Said you'd spoilt the evening, that's all.'

Fran nodded. Was *that* all? 'That's okay,' she said cautiously. 'I already knew that. Don't worry,' she said, and even managed a smile. 'I've let him rant on for a bit and get it out of his system. We've made it up.'

He looked at her closely with the seasoned eye of the man whose job it was to observe the behaviour of other human beings and the question seemed to come out all on its own. 'But that's not all you did, is it, Fran?'

Her feeling of relief evaporated as quickly as it had arrived. 'Are you asking me whether we had sex?'

Cormack was momentarily lost for words.

'Are you?'

'Er, yes—I suppose I am.'

'And why should it worry you so much if we did?'

He shook his head. 'It doesn't matter.'

Fran turned to him, her eyes full of distrust. 'Yes, it does. You know it does, so stop saying it doesn't! Tell me, Cormack. *Please*.' And then she aimed straight for the jugular. 'I mean, who out of the two of us do you think needs protecting most? Me—or Sam?'

Cormack hesitated only for a moment. 'He told me that he intended to pay you back for trying to make a fool of him.'

'And how was he going to do that?'

He sighed. 'I kind of got the idea that he was going to exact a form of payment which might be a mutually enjoyable experience....' His voice tailed off rather helplessly.

She gazed at him. 'Do you mean what I think you mean, Cormack? Or are you going to spell it out for me?'

'I took it to mean that he meant making love to you, yes.'

Had it all been a charade then? The closeness and communication she had thought existed between her and Sam. Had the sweet words and tender caresses of the night been nothing more than a sham?

She shook her head and turned away from him, not wanting Cormack to be witness to the betrayal and hurt in her eyes all over again. He had witnessed it with Sholto and Sholto had been her husband. So how come this new hurt seemed to wound her as nothing had before?

She waited until she was sure the threat of tears was at bay. 'Can you give me a lift to the station?' she asked him. 'And please don't spin me a line about hadn't I better see Sam first!'

'Fran—'

'Either you will, in which case I'd like to leave right now. Or you won't, so I'd need to call a taxi. And I'd prefer not to do that!'

There was a short silence while Cormack seemed to

weigh up his options against her determination. 'I'll give you a lift,' he agreed, at last. 'If only to know that you've boarded the train safely. But leave Sam a note, Fran. Please.'

She was tempted to tell him that she was in no mood to make bargains. 'Why should I?'

'Because otherwise he'll worry and go chasing after you and presumably, that's not what you want.' His eyes gleamed with a question. 'Or is it?'

'It's the last thing on earth I want,' she lied, and picked up a pen as if it were a sword. Her hands were trembling so much that she could barely write. 'But don't worry, Cormack,' she vowed grimly. 'I'll leave him a note he'll never forget!'

CHAPTER ELEVEN

THIS time Fran didn't go half way up a mountain to stay with her friends—she flew straight back to Dublin and stayed in her flat and waited.

And carried on waiting.

Then she tried to tell herself that she wasn't waiting at all. But that anyone would expect Sam to come running, under the circumstances. Even though her note had told him never to darken her door again.

But he didn't.

Which left Fran with no option but to try to sort out the tatters of her career and ultimately, her life. When she had left Ireland, people had been cancelling assignments right, left and centre. Her savings weren't *huge*, and she fully expected to have to go trawling round the employment agencies, looking for secretarial work to tide her over.

But she quickly discovered that people had very short memories and that offers of work, if not exactly flooding in, had certainly started trickling in steadily enough to provide an income. A old friend of Cormack's wanted a twenty-first birthday party arranged for his daughter. Through that came the request to organise a corporate function.

Fran found that she had enough work to keep herself busy and occupied...but there was a great, yawning space where her heart should have been.

Several times she lifted the telephone to ring him, and each time she slammed the receiver down with determined resolution. She had spent most of her time with Sholto overlooking his various betrayals. If she had learnt one lesson from her broken marriage it was that she was *not* going to be a doormat.

It was on a Sunday morning when Fran was wakened from a heavy sleep by the loud shrilling of the doorbell. She looked at the bedside clock. It had taken her hours to drop off last night and the plus side of having no social life was that she had blissfully imagined being able to sleep until noon. Or beyond.

She groped her hand out for the sun-gold dressing gown and struggled into it just as the doorbell shrilled again, and when she opened the door, there stood Sam. She stood there just gaping at him, swamping down her instinctive feeling of pleasure at seeing him. And replacing it with one of righteous indignation.

'Yes, Sam?'

'Can I come in?'

'Last time you didn't bother asking.'

'That was then.' His mouth flattened at the corners. 'This is now.'

She thought fleetingly that he didn't sound in the least bit apologetic. She opened the door with a shrug. 'Feel free.'

His mouth flattened even more and Fran could have cursed herself for her rather unfortunate choice of words.

They stood in the hallway, facing one another like two boxers in the ring, wariness and suspicion on both their faces. But Fran noticed one emotion which was clearly etched on *his* features.

Fury.

She studied him as coolly as she knew how. 'Well?'

'Have you always had such a problem with communication?' he queried, in a voice which was even colder than hers. 'Is that what helped your marriage to break down?'

She stared at him, not quite understanding.

'So that whenever there's a problem in your life, you bury your head in the sand—'

'I don't know what you're talking about!'

'By running away and refusing to discuss anything? Is that what you used to do with Sholto?'

'You leave Sholto out of this!' she flared. 'He has nothing to do with it!'

'Are you sure?' The blue eyes glittered. 'Aren't the sins of the first husband being revisited on every man who follows?'

She wasn't going to take this opportunity to point out that he was the *only* man who had followed. 'No. You have enough sins of your own, Sam.'

He seemed bemused. 'Then maybe you'd care to list them. Who knows, it might save me a visit to the analyst!'

She willed her voice to stay steady, to present the facts as clearly as she could, without resorting to hysteria. Which is what she felt like doing. 'It's quite simple.' She drew a deep breath. 'You were furious with me after the Valentine ball, weren't you?'

'That's hardly a state secret, Fran! I came here to tell you that myself if you remember!'

'And the deal was that I would come over to England and organise your mother's birthday—to make up for what happened?'

'That was the deal,' he agreed steadily.

'And for you to prove to me that I had fundamentally misjudged you, and that deep down you were a wonderful human being.'

'Wonderful? Hmmm. Maybe.' His eyes challenged

her. 'The choice of adjective was yours, remember, Fran.'

She shook her head. She wasn't going to let him flirt with her. 'But the truth was a lot more sinister, wasn't it, Sam? In fact, you were so angry that you decided you were going to get rid of that rage in a *very basic way indeed*.'

He raised his brows. 'You mean by making love to you?'

Fran shook her head. 'Oh, please don't dress it up! Certainly not for my sake! We had sex, Sam. *Sex!* Sex which you had planned. Cormack told me—'

'Cormack had no *right* to come to tell you—'

'He may not have had the *right*,' she echoed fiercely. 'But I'm bloody glad that he did!'

'Words which I said to him, in confidence and *in anger*, in the heat of the moment,' he emphasised slowly. 'And which were not intended for your ears. Ask yourself honestly, Fran, about what happened between us that night. It was good, wasn't it?'

She turned her head away.

'Very good?'

He caught her arm but she pushed him away.

'*Wasn't* it?'

'Yes,' she said at last, reluctantly.

'And did my actions seem like the actions of a man motivated only by anger? Or revenge?'

No, they didn't, and that was what was confusing her. 'Maybe you're good at faking it?' she suggested insultingly.

Sam took a slow, deep inhalation of air through his nostrils. 'I thought that was what women tended to do,' he murmured.

'I meant faking affection, not orgasm!' she snapped,

thinking that no woman would have to fake *anything* if they were in bed with a man like Sam. But she closed her mind to her thoughts. Too dangerous. 'You were as sweet as honey to me, Sam!' she accused. 'Luring me into your arms—'

'Don't make me out to be some sort of primitive caveman,' he said, in a weary voice. 'I got the distinct impression that you were in just the right mood to be lured.'

'That's not the point!'

'No? Then what exactly *is* your point?'

'Just that you're good at getting what you want. You wanted Rosie and you've had her—and now you've had me, too!' There was a long pause. 'Cold-bloodedly using a charm offensive to have your way with us! Just like she said!'

The pause which followed this statement was even longer.

'So you're not even going to deny it?' she questioned shrilly.

'No.'

Fran had expected emotion. A furious denial. The true story of how he had come to take Rosie's virginity. But there was nothing. Just a rather bland, disappointed look. As if he had reached the end of the line.

'Well, if that's what you really think about, then there's nothing more to be said. Is there?' He looked at her for a long, considering moment, and Fran wondered what he would have done if she had thrown herself into his arms and told him that they would forget everything which had happened in the past. And start anew.

Except that they couldn't. She knew they couldn't. The accusations lay like a great, gaping gulf between them.

'Goodbye, Fran,' he said quietly.

'Goodbye, Sam,' she answered, in a wooden voice, waiting until she could see his tall, black-haired figure striding off down the road before she allowed herself the luxury of dissolving into tears.

But the tears brought her no comfort, only the growing realization that she had made a huge mistake. She picked up the phone to try Rosie's number in London, but the line was busy.

She was standing staring out at the Dublin skyline, when the telephone started ringing and she snatched it up.

'Fran?'

Her heart sank with disappointment. No, not Sam at all. Better get used to it. 'Oh, it's you, Rosie. What do you want?'

'That's a *very* nice greeting for your oldest friend, isn't it? Especially as I know from pressing my callback button, that you've just been trying to ring me. Oh, the wonders of modern science!'

Fran didn't say anything, not right then. She needed to know the whole story about what had happened between Rosie and Sam, but she wasn't sure if she could bear to listen to it.

'Are you still there, Fran?'

'Yes. I'm still here.'

'Well, listen, I've got the *most* exciting news!'

Fran tried and failed to inject even one syllable with enthusiasm. 'Go on.'

'You know that the newspaper tried to find me my perfect man—well, they succeeded! And how! Fran, I'm *getting married*!'

There was a short pause while Fran digested this astonishing piece of news. 'But I thought...'

'What?'

'I thought you were still in love with Sam,' said Fran, from between gritted teeth.

'*Sam?*' Rosie chuckled. 'Oh, no! I *thought* I was, but I realise now that it was more a case of wounded pride, because he didn't want me the way I wanted him.' Her voice sobered suddenly. 'I suppose he told you what really happened between us?'

'Of course he didn't tell me!' said Fran icily. 'Even though I asked him, he wouldn't!'

Rosie sighed. 'That's par for the course. Loyal man. And it's been part of Sam's trouble all along. He's just too good for his own good!'

'Well, you've certainly changed your tune,' snapped Fran, thinking that there had been no mention of goodness when Rosie had first poured her heart out to her. She had had to find that out for herself... Her patience finally gave way. 'Listen, Rosie, why don't you tell me once and for all just what *did* happen between you and Sam? Only I want the truth this time.'

'What, *now*? On the telephone?'

'Unless you'd like to jump on a flight over to Dublin?'

There was a pause. 'I don't think you're going to like me very much....'

'Go on,' said Fran grimly.

'I was mad for him—we all were. But he just wasn't interested, not in me, or the others, not in anyone. He was still getting over Megan, you see. Er, you do know about his fiancée who died?'

'I do now!' said Fran furiously. 'It would have been a lot more helpful if I had known about her before, but of course it wasn't in your interests to tell me, was it, Rosie?'

'I'm sorry—'

'Just get on with the story!'

Rosie sounded even more shamefaced. 'Once I realised that he was immune to the normal feminine wiles, I decided to become his friend instead. I feel so bad about it now, Fran,' she moaned. 'The calculated, cold-blooded way I got him to rely on me as a good mate!'

Another pause.

'And?' asked Fran coldly.

'One night I got him drunk. Deliberately. Then I used every trick in the book to get him into bed. Oh, Fran, I'll never forget the look of disgust on his face the next morning. He couldn't even *remember* what had happened! I tried to get him out of my mind, but I just couldn't. And the trouble was that it was great sex, even though—'

'Please don't give me those kind of details!' shrieked Fran.

'My confidence was shot to pieces, my self-esteem at an all-time low. I felt that my life was suspended because I still wanted him so much. I just couldn't get him out of my system.' She sighed. 'The Valentine ball was my last-ditch attempt, but I knew it was hopeless, even before I saw him dancing with you. The others thought that he really liked you.'

'I actually think that he did,' said Fran sadly. 'But it's too late now.'

'Are you sure?'

Fran was not in the mood for telling Rosie that he had just left, uttering the most final-sounding goodbye she had ever heard in her life. Because she had chosen to listen to the story of a scorned woman, instead of what she knew in her heart to be true. 'Quite sure,' she said crisply.

'Fran, just let me tell you something else.'

'What?' Fran's voice was wary.

'You know he kissed you on the dance floor?'

'What about it?'

'Well, that was when I realised that there was no hope any more. And that's what made me so reckless, I think. You see, he never kissed me, Fran, not once. Even though I shared his bed for the night.'

Fran swallowed as her mind tried to work out the implications of this. No kissing. Sex without tenderness. The opposite of what she had shared with him. 'Listen, Rosie, I have to go——'

'But don't you want to hear about the man I'm going to marry?'

Perhaps she should have chosen just that moment to tell Rosie that she was probably the most insensitive person in the world, but Fran didn't have the heart. Surely one person who was hurting this badly was enough to be with?

'Not now,' she said. 'I have something I need to do.'

After she had put the phone down, she paced round the flat, trying to put herself in Sam's place. Would he have flown straight back to London? Or booked into a hotel? And if so, which hotel?

She ran over to her address book where she had all the hotels listed, and started with the best, hardly able to believe her luck when they informed her that yes, Mr. Lockhart had a reservation, and that yes, they would try to find him for her, but they thought that he might be in the process of checking out, if he hadn't already done so.

Well, she wasn't going to give him the opportunity.

'If you see him—tell him to wait!' Fran puffed.

She ran straight out of the flat and into the street where she hailed a taxi. The driver pulled over, giving

her a rather funny look and she wondered why until she
realised that she was still in her gold-satin kimono! She
looked down at it in horror for a moment, and then
shrugged her shoulders. What the heck, she thought.
This was Ireland, after all!

'Get me to the Sherbourne, quick!' she demanded.
'Break as many speed limits as you like, just don't hurt
anyone on the way!'

'Right!' grinned the driver, who looked as though he
had spent his entire life waiting for someone to say just
that to him!

The Sherbourne was opulent and grand without being
in the least bit stuffy, but even so Fran raised more than
a few eyebrows as she rushed inside, tightening the gold-
satin sash around her waist as she did so.

'Can I help you?' asked the receptionist, giving an
almost imperceptible look of alarm in the direction of
one of the burly doormen.

'I'd like to see Mr. Sam Lockhart,' said Fran. 'Please.'

'And is he expecting you?'

Fran indicated her rather unconventional attire. 'Well,
hardly!'

The receptionist ran her eyes down a list in front of
her. 'I think he may have already checked out—'

'So I have,' came a deep voice and Fran spun round
to find a pair of sapphire eyes studying her with some
bemusement.

'Sam!' she cried. 'Oh, Sam!'

The receptionist was now obviously sizing the two of
them up and had decided there was no way that someone
like Sam would wish to be bothered with someone like
Fran.

'I'm sorry if you've been bothered, Mr. Lockhart,' she
said, with a flash of her green eyes which was a little

bit more familiar than it needed to be. She looked disapprovingly at Fran, who was hastily re-knotting the belt on her kimono. 'I can arrange to have security come and—'

Sam shook his dark head. 'No, that's fine,' he smiled. 'Miss Fisher and I will be sitting over there—' He gestured with his head to where tables were grouped in the high-ceilinged foyer, where people had been drinking morning coffee and sliding scrumptious cakes onto bone china plates, but were now momentarily distracted by the sight of Fran. 'Perhaps you could arrange to have a tray of tea sent over in a little while?'

'Certainly, sir.'

Fran felt his hand firmly grip her elbow and propel her towards a vacant table. 'Come and sit down,' he murmured. 'Or are you enjoying drawing this much attention to yourself?'

All her courage seemed to have suddenly deserted her. 'I must look a sight,' she muttered.

'A fairly distracting sight,' he agreed. 'Come on. That table over in the corner is free, and it's right out of the way.'

She was glad to sink down in a chair, away from all the curious faces. Then she forced herself to look into the dark-blue eyes, expecting to find bitterness and recrimination there, but was astonished to find none. Just that wry, questioning look.

'You aren't angry with me any more?' she said.

'Should I be?' He settled back in the chair watchfully. 'My anger is all spent, Fran. Interested is the word I would use to describe my reaction to seeing you here dressed in that extraordinary outfit. No, scrub that. Intrigued.'

She took a deep breath. This wasn't going to be easy,

and neither was she expecting it to be easy. So it was important that she expressed herself in a way which made it clear that there could be no misunderstanding.

'I'm so sorry, Sam,' she said simply. 'Really, really sorry.'

If she had stood up and performed a slow and erotic striptease, Sam could not have been more surprised.

'*You're* sorry?' His eyes narrowed. 'Why?'

'For allowing myself to be drawn into this whole stupid saga—this childish quest for revenge, without bothering to find out whether it was justified.'

He digested this for a moment. 'And what's brought all this on?'

'Rosie rang me—' she bit her lip.

'And?'

'And told me the truth about your encounter with her—'

'The *whole* truth?' he frowned.

'Well, not all the gory details. She said she'd got you drunk.' She looked at him with a question in her eyes.

Sam sighed. He had tried to do the decent thing by not telling her what had really happened that night, but suddenly he realised that his well-meaning courtesy had been badly misplaced. Half-truths bred like bacteria in the fertile breeding ground of the imagination and he needed to exorcise the knock-on effects of the whole sorry incident before it did any more harm.

'She caught me at a vulnerable time,' he said slowly. 'It had been the second anniversary of Megan's death, and I couldn't face the thought of going home to an empty flat. Rosie was working at Gordon-Browne with me, always the listener, always attentive. But she wasn't in-my-face, like the other four. She had become a friend. Or so I thought.'

'Yes. She said.'

'That night she insisted that I needed to get out more, said that she'd take me to a wine-bar she knew for a quick drink on the way home.'

Fran nodded.

'The quick drink turned into a long drink. A very long drink. I was already quite smashed when we got into a cab and headed for my flat. I should have eaten something and crashed out and woken up with an almighty headache, but I allowed Rosie to persuade me to drink some whisky.' His eyes were very blue and very troubled. 'I have only vague recollections of what happened during the night, but my memory of the morning is much clearer. Rosie told me that we'd made love during the night, and that she had been a virgin.' His mouth twisted with horror and pain.

'I'm not trying to absolve myself of all the blame—obviously there must have been a part of me that wanted it to happen, otherwise, I presume I wouldn't have been capable.'

'Don't!' she whispered.

'I have to, honey.' He swallowed down the self-disgust he felt. 'I tried to feel something for Rosie, but I simply couldn't. Then when she let slip that she had been determined to have me, and had manoeuvred me into that position…well, I found that I didn't even want to see her any more. From being a friend whom I relied on she became the symbol of a night when I felt I'd sunk so low, I wasn't sure I'd ever be able to rise to the surface again.'

'But you did,' she said softly.

Sam reeled, taken aback by her generosity. 'Yes, I did. But I also knew that I needed space. And solitude. After that night I decided that I was going to leave London and leave Gordon-Browne, and work from home, and that's what I did. I said sorry and goodbye to Rosie, and that—I thought—was that. It was so long ago. I can't believe she let it fester all this time.'

Fran nodded. She suspected that Sam had little idea of his real impact on the opposite sex. She also suspected that Rosie had not exactly lived like a nun in the ensuing years. 'The most attractive thing in the world is often the thing you know you can't have.'

'You look pretty attractive to me right now,' he said softly, a question in his eyes.

She thought of what he'd said about her inability to communicate, and knew that his words had more than a grain of truth in them. 'Well, you can have me any time you want me,' she smiled softly. 'You know you can.'

He leaned across, took her hand in his and raised it to his mouth. 'Oh, Fran,' he said, and his breath felt warm and alive against her skin. 'Don't you realise that I've fallen hopelessly in love with you?'

'Oh, not *hopelessly*!' she flirted. 'Because I love you, too.'

Sam felt a tug of desire so overwhelming that he felt dizzy with the anticipation of it. 'No, not hopelessly,' he murmured.

'Rosie also told me—'

He groaned. 'Oh, honey! Haven't we exhausted the subject of Rosie yet?'

'That she was getting married—'

'Well, that's nice,' he said evenly. 'In fact, that's *wonderful*—to use one of your favourite adjectives. I'm not really interested in the details—certainly not now—but we'll send them a wedding present that's simply—'

'Wonderful!' she giggled, but her eyes were wide with question. 'You aren't angry with her?'

Sam shrugged. 'What's the point? Anger is such a waste of time. And anyway, I've got the woman of my dreams.' His brows lifted in delicate query. 'At least, I *think* I have? But maybe we should go somewhere more private, and discuss the question in some detail?'

'But you've just checked out,' she objected.

'So I have.' Sam smiled, but there was hunger in his eyes as he held out a hand towards her. 'I guess that means we'd better jump in a cab and go straight back to your flat, hadn't we, honey?'

CHAPTER TWELVE

'TWINS,' said Sam slightly unsteadily. *'Twins!'*

'Well, don't sound so shocked, darling,' said Fran demurely. 'When a couple spends so much time making love without using any form of protection then a pregnancy is almost certainly on the cards, wouldn't you say?'

'But *twins*,' he said again, in a dazed voice. 'Fran, honey. Two of everything—two cots, two high chairs, two car-seats—'

'Two babies,' she reminded him.

'Are you scared?'

'Terrified. And I've never been happier!'

'Haven't you?'

She heard the faint trace of wistfulness in his voice, and knew what had caused it. In the two years since they had been married, their happiness rating seemed to have almost shot off the scale. Particularly since they had decided to make their main home on the coast, just outside Dublin, where the beautiful blue sweep of the bay lulled you into thinking you were in the Mediterranean.

'I've been so happy with you, and it just gets better and better,' she told him gently. 'And the babies will only add to that happiness.'

'I know they will.' He raised her hand to his mouth and pressed it against his lips. 'It's just that I've had you all to myself and I know that you're going to be the most fantastic mother in the world, and—'

'And what?' she prompted softly.

186

'I'm going to have to share you now.' He raised his dark brows. 'Is that a terrible thing to say?'

Fran grinned. 'No, it's a wonderful thing to say. It means that we communicate honestly with one another and that's more priceless than gold-dust. Besides, don't you think I've thought it, too?'

'Honestly?'

'Honestly! Don't you know that every single positive event has a negative aspect to it? Our babies are going to be the most wonderful babies ever to be born, but we'd be fools if we closed our minds to some of the things which happen when you have them.'

His eyes were tender. 'Such as?'

'Well, babies make you tired. And put you off sex—'

'Oh, really?' he teased softly.

'Well, I can't quite see that happening,' she admitted, and blushed.

'No.' He lifted her chin and looked at her with love. At the soft green sweater which made her eyes look like bay leaves, and the sexy white jeans she wore. Her hair hung shimmering almost to her waist.

Fran had recognised that she had evolved a style of dressing to balance her husband's theatrical image. Now she didn't have to do that any more. The sensible, neutral clothes had gone. She had thrown off the shackles of her former life, and she was free to just be Fran Lockhart.

'Twins!' he said again, only now the smile on his face had broken into an unfettered grin and he picked her up in his arms and began to kiss her over and over again, while outside the waves of the Irish sea lapped like music beneath them.

London's streets aren't just paved with gold—they're home to three of the world's most eligible bachelors!

You can meet these gorgeous men, and the women who steal their hearts, in:

NOTTING HILL GROOMS

Look out for these tantalizing romances set in London's exclusive Notting Hill, written by highly acclaimed authors who, between them, have sold more than 35 million books worldwide!

Irresistible Temptation by Sara Craven
Harlequin Presents® #2077
On sale December 1999

Reform of the Playboy by Mary Lyons
Harlequin Presents® #2083
On sale January 2000

The Millionaire Affair by Sophie Weston
Harlequin Presents® #2089
On sale February 2000

Available wherever Harlequin books are sold.

HARLEQUIN®
Makes any time special ™

HARLEQUIN PRESENTS®

Seduction
~~SWEET REVENGE~~

They wanted to get even.
Instead they got...married!

by bestselling author

Penny Jordan

Don't miss Penny Jordan's latest enthralling miniseries about four special women. Kelly, Anna, Beth and Dee share a bond of friendship and a burning desire to avenge a wrong. But in their quest for revenge, they each discover an even stronger emotion.
Love.

Look out for all four books in Harlequin Presents®:

November 1999
THE MISTRESS ASSIGNMENT

December 1999
LOVER BY DECEPTION

January 2000
A TREACHEROUS SEDUCTION

February 2000
THE MARRIAGE RESOLUTION

Available at your favorite retail outlet.

HARLEQUIN®
Makes any time special ™

HPSRS